Highland Oath

Book One

Highland Treasures

highland oath

highland treasures

book one

by

c.a. szarek

Paper Dragon Publishing

Highland Oath
C.A. Szarek

Highland Treasures Book One

Paper Dragon Publishing
North Richland Hills, TX

eBook ISBN: 978-1-941151-33-4
Print book ISBN: 978-1-941151-34-1

Published in the United States of America

First eBook Edition: November, 2017
First Print Edition: January, 2018

Second eBook Edition: September, 2023
Second Print Edition: September, 2023

other books by c.a. szarek

<u>Highland Secrets Trilogy & Companions—</u>
<u>Historical Fantasy Romance</u>
The Princess and The Laird (Highland Secrets Prequel)
The Tartan MP3 Player (Book One)
The Fae Ring (Book Two)
The Parchment Scroll (Book Three)
Highland Valentine (A Highland Secrets HEA Story)
Highlander's Portrait (A Highland Secrets Story)

<u>Highland Treasures—Historical Fantasy Romance</u>
Highland Oath (Book One)
Highland Essence (Book Two)
Highland Skies (Book Three)

<u>The King's Riders—Fantasy Romance</u>
Sword's Call (Book One)—*Also in Audio*
Love's Call (Book Two)—*Also in Audio*
Rogue's Call (Book Three)—*Also in Audio*
Fate's Call (A Novella from the World of the King's Riders)—*Also in Audio*

<u>Crossing Forces — Romantic Suspense</u>
Collision Force (Book One) — *Also in Audio*
Cole in Her Stocking (A Crossing Forces Christmas) — *FREE read!*
Chance Collision (Book Two) — *Also in Audio*
Calculated Collision (Book Three) — *Also in Audio*
Collision Control (Book Four) — *Also in Audio*
Weekend Collision (A Crossing Forces HEA Story) — *FREE read!*
Superior Collision (Book Five) — *Also in Audio*
Incendiary Collision (Book Six) — *Coming Soon!*

<u>The Giovanni</u>
King of Hearts (Book One) — *Also in Audio*
Queen of Diamonds (Book Two) — *Coming Soon!*

Dedication

To all the Scotophiles out there who dream of real time travel and tall, very hot, muscled men in kilts. (Just without the smelly realities of the past).

chapter one

ngus was too late.

The gush of magic raced through the air, even up on the high overhanging ridge when he skidded his horse to a halt and threw his leg over her wide back. He slid down Magda's side and didn't stop to pat or thank the red roan mare.

Another surge, thrown like a pulsating shield, hit his senses and he bit back curses. He scrambled down the cliff-face, clinging before he jumped to the loamy beach, so he wouldn't fall in his haste. Last thing he needed was a black and blue arse — or worse, an injury like his da's.

His foolish *foolish* lass of a sister and his idiot cousin had already opened the Faery Stones. His mother had been right. Even though the dangers of the Fae were well known by the lad and lass, they'd acted unwisely, impulsively.

Recklessly.

Fear inched in on the edges of his vision, but he tried to stave it off.

I really am too late.

What if they were harmed…or killed by a race of people who considered them enemies, no matter they had shared blood?

Angus' heart sank to his gut. His family would never survive their loss. His father and uncles would wage war if their children were lost, no matter the risk.

His strong draw to the magic Stones scattered his dark thoughts and made his blood thrum the closer he got.

Waves crashed into the beach, sounding as loud and angry as he felt, but he paid them no heed. He stormed into the cave that housed the magical portal.

It led to the Realm of the Fae, but with someone who wasn't wholly of Fae blood — as was the case with all *three* of them — it often could rip open a doorway in time, usually the far far future.

Even before he reached the place inside where the meager entrance widened into a cavern, the Faery Stones called to his magic, humming in welcome, an audible tune in his head. Angus tried to ignore the plea, its power, and focus on the two misfits before him, but the Faery Stones demanded their due, as if claiming the part of him that was Fae.

Five large crystals sat atop five natural-looking rock-like formations on the cave floor, in a semi-circle that looked too perfect to be accidental placement. They were lit from the inside, an almost throbbing radiance, and in turn, illuminated the cave.

They'd been grown, curated with magic, but not by humans. His mother, a former Fae princess, speculated the Faery Stones had been brought to the

Human Realm a millennia ago by curious Fae who wanted to explore their sister realm.

The cave containing the magical gate wasn't overly large, but it wasn't tiny, and the natural floor was littered with starkly white sand, much different than outside on the pebble-ridden beach.

He stilled, eyes landing on a diminutive dark-haired lass, and a broad-shouldered lad standing next to her. His cousin's height and breadth belied his youth of eight and ten years.

Like most MacLeod males, they both towered over his sister. She wasn't the height of Liam's mother, their Aunt Janet; Alexandria was only a few inches past five feet.

They stood next to the crystals, their collective gaze looking from him to the Stones and back. The portal wasn't in sight—it must've closed already.

Then why did the double measure of trouble stand there in front of him?

Angus had assumed he'd have to traverse to the Fae Realm to go after them—or worse, into the future.

What'd kept them in the cave?

How much time has passed?

Maybe they hadn't been able to open the Stones?

The magic he'd felt disagreed. There'd been too much present for a failed attempt.

Angus glared.

His younger sister winced.

Good, she was properly a'feared, even though he

had yet to speak. He cleared his throat and told himself to breathe.

Perhaps things weren't as bad as his mother had dreaded. At least he didn't have to go into danger *alone* to retrieve them.

"What have ye ta say fer yerselves?" he demanded.

Again, the pair looked at each other, mute.

Quite unusual for his little pest of a sister.

Angus narrowed his eyes. "Speak. An' be glad 'tis I standin' here, instead of our mother. Or yer father, Liam." He looked at each of them pointedly.

Light from the Stones revealed pink cheeks on both culprits.

Alexandria was dressed not in a fine gown as the lady she was by birth, but in trews and an oversized ivory leine she'd no doubt stolen from a male relative's trunk—maybe even his own. The tight breeches fit well; the purple fabric denoted they probably belonged to their mother.

The lad wore attire like Angus' own—a MacLeod plaid belted on and a saffron leine. At least he'd brought his sword, but it wouldn't help against Fae magic.

"I..." Angus' sister said, then nothing more.

"*We* are Fae, too," Liam said.

Angus frowned. "Meanin'?"

Alexandria squared her thin shoulders. "We've a right ta tha Faery Stones, as much as ye an' *Màthair*."

"The Stones dinnae be playthings. The Fae are dangerous," he said.

"So everaone always says," his sister muttered.

He growled and took a step closer, intentionally looming over her. "Ye ken *better* than ta doubt *Màthair* and Xander's words. Yer *selfish!* Da is hurt, *badly*, and here ye are, playin' games ye ken nothin' about!" He wanted to grab and shake her.

Her violet eyes—just like their mother's—widened. "Da's hurt?" Her expression melted into something concerned, but that didn't fix a damn thing in Angus' eyes.

"He was tossed from his horse comin' after ye! Broke his leg, an' 'tis bad, lass." He didn't soften his voice. Angus didn't know how bad just yet, their mother had ordered him to keep going; to go as far as he needed to.

He'd seen blood. The bone had protruded from their father's shin.

In his peripheral vision, their cousin was pacing. "Liam, what do *ye* have ta say fer yerself?" he repeated his demand.

The lad shook his head, and his dark curly hair fell into his violet eyes. He shoved it back and exchanged another look with Lexi that Angus didn't miss.

His sister had been dubbed '*Lexi*' by their Aunt Claire, who'd come from the far future and married their father's twin, Uncle Duncan, some twenty years before.

Every last MacLeod usually called her the nickname—except their mother.

"Yer da stayed with ours, but he's less than pleased wit' ye."

His cousin was still young enough to blush deeper. Liam looked down, studying his boots. "I just wanted ta fly," he whispered.

Angus blew out a breath. "The Fae dinnae take kindly ta humans, even if we're all only half. They woulda killed ye, lad. Without remorse or delay. Ye *both* know tha'."

"I have wings there, like my da."

Alarm rushed over Angus' form and his hands twitched. He kept them at his sides instead of strangling the younger man. "*How* do ye ken tha'?"

"I've gone there a' fore…I've flown."

Lexi was a brighter red now, and they exchanged yet another look.

They'd always been close, but the nonverbal communication was a bit much. It was getting under Angus' skin. To think *he* was usually the calm, even-tempered one, like his father. He was acting more like his Uncle Duncan, but then again, the lad and lass had given him cause.

He wanted to rant and rave. Pace and lecture like children deserved. However, they *weren't* wee ones anymore. His sister was nine and ten—of marrying age—and Liam was right behind her, a year younger.

They'd been warned their whole lives of the danger of the Fae since they all had a full-blooded Fae parent. Besides, hollering at Lexi never worked.

Their father always said she was much like their mother in that regard. They'd been born of a Fae princess — so their blood was legitimately royal in the other realm.

He sighed and rammed his hand through his long hair, wincing when his fingers found a wind-induced tangle. Angus took a turn of pacing in front of the Faery Stones, trying to compose himself instead of shouting the chaos in his head.

Lexi and Liam stood side-by-side, remaining unusually silent.

Awareness of…*something*…darted down his spine. Angus whirled and tilted his chin up, studying them with narrowed eyes.

As soon as his sister spared him a glance, she quickly averted her gaze, and their cousin's was downcast at his boots again. Guilt rolled off them both; he could *feel* it, and he wasn't an empath like his mother.

"What dinnae ye be tellin' me?" He swallowed, half-fearing the answer.

Lexi took a big breath and glimpsed their cousin once more before meeting Angus head-on. "Somethin' — some*one* — came through tha portal."

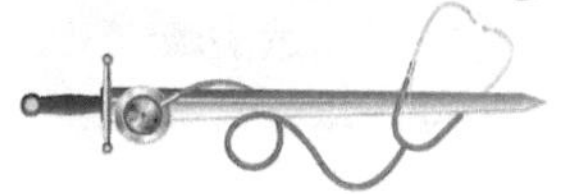

Lila smiled at Lizzie's laughter and jogged to catch up with her friends.

"What's wrong? You cannae keep up, America?" Sophie winked, and her thick Scottish accent rolled over her senses.

It'd taken time to get used to it, but a year into her three-year fellowship, and she finally didn't have trouble understanding everyone. Handy, since she needed to be completely clear in the operating room.

At first, Lila had been offended by the pretty redhead's nickname for her, but there was affection, not distain, when the Scottish doctor nicknamed Lila her country of origin.

Then again, she'd been born in Mexico and her family had moved to Texas when she was an infant, so she was both Mexican *and* American.

"Come, Lila!" Lizzie called, grinning and flashing dimples.

The blonde nurse was so sweet, and the first person at the hospital who'd welcomed the surgeon that had come from so far away. She was English, not Scottish, but had lived in Edinburgh since she'd been a teen. "The group's gonna get inside Dunvegan before we do!"

"Coming!" Lila closed some distance of rocky beach to rejoin them. The day was warm, but the wind was chilly, blowing her hair in her face, and making the fabric of her light jacket flap. She fought a shiver; perhaps she should've layered and worn a sweater, too. "Did you get all the shots you wanted?" she asked Sophie, who was a budding photographer as well as a doctor.

The redhead grinned and held up her expensive fancy camera. "Aye. Though I'd like one of the three of us."

Lizzie's face lit up and her blue eyes sparkled. Her fair locks danced around her face, making her appear young and innocent. "Oh, of course! I'll ask someone when we rejoin the tour group."

Lila looked out at the waters again. "I love this place. Skye is so peaceful." She noticed Sophie's nod from the corner of her eye.

"We used ta come up here when I was wee." She'd grown up on a sheep farm right outside of Inverness, and proudly spoke of her Highlander ancestry.

Over the last year, these two women had become her closest friends. They'd decided to have a weekend getaway and had traveled from Edinburgh where they worked at the hospital. They'd stayed with Sophie's family the night before and had taken a day-trip to the Hebrides, and were going to tour several castles all over the Western Isles.

The stronghold of Clan MacLeod — Dunvegan — was first on the menu. The building was over seven centuries old.

When they'd arrived on the Isle of Skye as a group, they'd been given time to look around, and had headed down to the beach.

Sophie had wanted to snap some pictures.

Lila reached for her Saint Luke medal. Her grandmother had given it to her when she'd graduated from medical school.

She'd run her thumb over the engraved surface so many times for comfort. It was white gold, and one side depicted the Catholic patron saint of the medical profession and gospel author; the other side displayed a caduceus.

Her fingers failed to enclose on the familiar piece of jewelry. She looked down and unzipped her jacket. Felt inside her shirt but couldn't locate the fine chain.

"What's wrong?" Lizzie asked.

Lila's stomach jumped and she swallowed her rising panic. "My necklace." She looked at the loamy ground at her feet, then started retracing her steps down the beach. *Thank God* they weren't that close to the water, she might have a chance to spot it.

I have to find it.

"Did you have it on the bus?" Sophie asked sensibly.

Both friends had followed and were also studying the terrain.

"Positive," she said, meeting the fellow doctor's green eyes.

"Aye, ye have it on in this photo."

She spared a glance for the camera's small digital display in her friend's hands. Sure enough, the chain peeked out of her jacket, visible on her neck in the picture. Lila looked free and happy on the little screen, her dark hair with wind in it. The smile on her face felt far away as her gut churned.

The necklace was all she had left of her grandmother, her sweet *abuelita.*

It couldn't be gone.

"I have to find it." Her voice came out more of a whine, but she didn't look up. "My *lita* gave it to me, and—"

Lizzie grabbed both her hands and Lila met her concerned cornflower blue eyes. "We'll help. I know what it means to you."

Lila tried to blow out a breath of relief, but her middle was still in knots. She forced a nod and made her way down the beach, staring at every cluster of rocks, big and small. She scanned the surface of the sand and pebbles, willing her necklace to appear.

How could she have lost it?

She hadn't felt it fall off, so it could be *anywhere.*

Something glinted in the sunlight on the gritty ground ahead of her, so she jogged closer. Her heart leapt when she took in the embossed likeness of Saint Luke and bent to grab it.

Lila brushed the surface off, squeezed it in her fist, and held the pendant to her chest. "Thank you, God. I'm sorry, *Lita.* I didn't lose it!" She glanced over her shoulder.

Her friends were a ways back, and she looked up

at a ridge that rose above her head and hid the sun. It threw a long shadow toward the water, and the image of long grasses that must cover it swayed like ghosts in the moving air.

She didn't remember coming this far down, but she must've if her necklace was here. Lila ran the chain through her fingers to wipe the last of the sand away. The clasp was broken and hung open, never to be joined with the other side again. "Damn," she whispered. Lila whirled around and waved her arms. "It's broken, but I found it!" She'd take it to a jewelry store when they got back to Edinburgh and get it fixed. If it wasn't repairable, she could always replace the chain.

"Oh good!" Lizzie yelled through her cupped hands.

Flashing a smile, she put her hand on the cliff-face beside her and pushed off, ready to jog back to her friends. Her body finally loosened, and her necklace was safely in her fist. She didn't want to shove it in her pocket, for fear she'd lose it again.

Sea spray hit her face and she winced as the wind picked up, gale strength from nowhere. Lila couldn't see, because her hair smacked her cheeks, poking at her eyes like repeated whips; she stumbled over the rocky surface at her feet.

Sophie called her name, and maybe Lizzie, too, but the sounds were ripped away by what felt like a tornado, pushing her backwards until she slammed into something behind her.

Pain exploded in her upper back and between her shoulder blades.

It was a boulder, a huge one next to the cliff she'd touched moments before.

Lila tried to move away, planting her feet, and using it as leverage, but she couldn't gain any purchase, despite her hiking boots. She screamed, but the noise was torn from her mouth, and her body lifted from the ground.

Then, the world went black.

chapter two

You cannot kill them.

Angus had to keep telling himself that. He bit down until his gums, teeth, and jaw ached in protest. "What?" The demand came out low and deadly.

His sister and cousin both stiffened, then squared their shoulders.

Good.

Let them be alarmed; scared. Even terrified would work to his favor.

"'Twas…a…lass." Liam's voice cracked as if he was a lad about to become a man, instead of the young adult he actually was. He gripped the hilt of his sword and flexed his fingers, but his hand shook.

At another time, Angus might've laughed, or inquired if his cousin was going to pull the weapon and attack.

Lexi shifted on her feet. "She…was…thrown ta the beach."

He glared at the fools before him for the hundredth time since he'd rushed into the cave. "An' ye dinnae think ta go after her?"

"Weel, ye came an' —" his cousin said.

"Jesu, lad. The lass shoulda been tha first thing

ou' of yer mouths!" Angus yelled, then darted out of the cavern. He stumbled through the small slit that posed as an entrance. It was narrow and he was large. A sharp edge caught his leine. He pulled away, ignoring the tearing sound that followed.

He needed to find the lass, now.

How had he not seen her when he'd arrived up on the ridge?

No movement on the beach below had caught his attention. Then again, he'd been focused on getting inside the Cave of the Faery Stones.

Likely, the new arrival wasn't from 1692. Time travel was disorienting, she could wander into the waters and drown. Worse, traversing the centuries relieved one of their clothing, so she would be out of sorts *and* naked.

The rush of steps behind him told Angus Lexi and Liam had followed, but they could catch up if they wanted; he wouldn't wait for them.

He dashed down the beach, but he didn't have to go far.

Angus saw a perfectly formed arse first. Then, long ebony hair flying about even though she was bent at the waist, both hands buried in the rocky sand, struggling to her feet. Her knees didn't seem to be assisting her; they wobbled as she attempted to adjust her stance.

"Quickly, get tha plaid off my horse," he barked at Liam.

His cousin disappeared up the ridge.

The lass finally pushed upright. She whirled around, shoving dancing locks from her face with one hand.

Angus should look away from her exposed breasts, but he couldn't. They were full, large, and her nipples were peaked—likely from the chill in the April air. His gaze wandered lower, taking in the tight *short* curls guarding her secrets at the apex of her thighs. Much less hair there than a woman of his time usually had.

Her long and slender legs were an odd combination of muscular and delicate; so appealing his mouth went dry. Every inch of her body was perfection, from slightly rounded hips and the soft part of her belly above her sex.

The lass' skin wasn't creamy alabaster like his sister's. It was darker; light brown toned, gorgeous.

Angus could've demanded the plaid off his cousin's back, but somehow it was important that he wrapped her in his own.

Makes no sense.

"She's bare as a bairn," Lexi squeaked beside him.

He scowled. "Aye, dinnae stare. This is *yer* fault."

His sister glared and perched her hands on her hips. "Ye alreada hollered a' me. An' 'twas *ye* tha' was starin, brother!" She smirked when their gazes brushed.

This attitude was more like his younger sibling than the somberness from the cave, but heat still kissed his neck at her correct observations. He'd stared at the naked time traveler.

Angus growled, and without sparing another look for Lexi, darted forward, blocking the view of the garmentless lass with his body. For some reason, he didn't want his cousin to see her nudity. At least his sister and the disoriented female had the same parts.

Not that he'd want to see Lexi in the same state of undress.

Liam skittered into view, wobbling as he halted with too much momentum.

Angus threw his arm out without comment, and his cousin thrust the MacLeod plaid into his waiting fingers. He wrapped the fabric around their new companion, squeezing her shoulders. "Lass?" He kept his voice low and gentle.

She looked up at him, but her big brown eyes were obviously hazy, unfocused. She wavered on her feet, despite his hold.

The beauty of her face stole his breath. Her cheekbones were high, her mouth full and her face heart shaped. Like the rest of her, everything was *perfect*.

He shook her gently. "Lass? Can ye see me?"

She went lax in his grip and closed her eyes.

Angus barely kept her from falling. He cursed and threw another dark look at his sister and their cousin. "This is yer fault," he snarled as he gathered the lass closer and lifted her into his arms.

He wouldn't be able to climb the ridge holding her, so he'd have to go the long way — down the beach, following the natural incline, then doubling back to Magda.

It took longer than he wanted to allow.

His mare snorted when he put the lass on her back, but he ignored her and swung himself behind the unconscious time traveler, pulling her into his chest before she could list to the side or topple over.

Angus had a hard time tearing his eyes from her face as she slept in his arms as if it was the most natural thing in the world. Granted, she'd passed out, but her expression was peaceful, angelic.

Her dark lashes were long, forming attractive half-moons on her high cheekbones, and she was flushed pink, probably from the cool wind on exposed skin.

It was almost as if, even in her repose, she begged for his lips on hers, but he didn't dare.

If wasn't as if she belonged to him.

The notion had Angus calling himself a delusional fool.

He hadn't often seen anyone with her warm brown skin tone, and he wanted to explore every inch of her, see if she was as soft as she looked.

One of her fists peeked out of his plaid, and it was closed tight, as if holding something.

Angus gently pried her hand open, and a thin chain with an oval pendant tumbled into his waiting fingers. The clasp on the piece of jewelry was broken—it was a wonder she hadn't lost it in her journey. He tucked it into his belt-pouch. He'd return the keepsake later.

He glanced back at her face. His sleeping charge hadn't stirred despite the retrieval. He let his eyes trace every visible inch of her beauty. His plaid enclosed her like a cape, and he regretted that she was no longer bared to him, as much as it made him a scoundrel.

Angus didn't know her. That, if nothing else, shouted he had no right to gaze upon her nudity. He'd always considered himself a man of honor, yet he'd stared at her on the beach as if he'd never seen a naked lass.

"What're ye doin'?"

His sister's voice made him jump and Magda must've caught his discomfort. She neighed and hoofed the dirt.

He tore his eyes from his new charge and cleared his throat. Had no reason to be embarrassed. Or feel as if he was a lad caught doing something wrong.

Lexi and Liam stood side-by-side not far up on the ridge. They were staring at him, and his sister had one slender dark eyebrow arched.

He'd not heard their ascent, which was startling. His neck heated, as it had when his younger sibling had observed his attention on the naked lass. "Hie ta Dunvegan," he ordered. Angus squeezed his knees into his mount's sides and left without making sure his recalcitrant sister and their cousin followed.

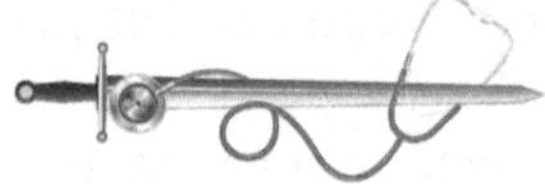

Lila was warm. She smiled and burrowed into the heat source, but it was hard; sure, as hell didn't feel like her pillow. A scent tickled her nose, and she wiggled. Not a bad smell; it was clean, rather masculine, and unfamiliar.

Sandalwood?

Her *lita* had always been into herbs and spices, and that was the closest thing it reminded her of. Even though she'd never agreed to her grandmother's holistic approach to healing, or opinions on medicines, some of the supplies she'd always had on hand smelled nice.

"At ease, lass. Be still, lest ye fall."

The voice was deep and had Lila obeying without delay. The grasp around her tightened, and sensations rolled over her body.

Someone was *holding* her.

Her eyes fluttered open, but it took several tries for her vision to focus. Gray clouds moved overhead, along with grassy hills. She — they — were moving?

"Am I on a horse?" What she'd meant as an incredulous demand came out as a whisper, and Lila cleared her dry throat.

"Aye."

She tried to right herself because she was half-laying across his lap, and he helped.

A large hand landed at the small of her back and she shivered. Something rather coarse brushed her skin, and her feet were cold.

Lila flexed her toes and glanced down. They were bare—no shoes, or socks.

What the hell?

Her legs peeked out from a plaid blanket wrapped around her like a bath towel. The visible expanse of her shins told her she wore no pants, either.

Where are my jeans?

Lila pulled the fabric away from her chest, inspecting beneath it.

"Why am I *naked?*" she yelped but couldn't muster any more embarrassment than had already washed over her. She locked eyes with the stranger.

They were blue—oh so blue—and she read sympathy there.

He was handsome, too. Long straight nose, full lips. Beardless cheeks and sable locks kissed his shoulders, making his bright eyes stand out even more. His cheeks were angled, as if sculpted.

"I'll explain everathin' when we get back ta Dunvegan, lass."

The brogue wasn't shocking—she'd been in Scotland for a year now, but the thickness was different from how Sophie sounded somehow, and it was smooth, rolling over her skin like a caress.

Lila trembled and fidgeted in his grip.

"Are ye cold?"

"My feet are." Words tumbled out of her mouth, but her thoughts scattered when the big hand on her back moved in slow circles. Despite the thick itchy fabric, heat radiated into her muscles, tempting, comforting. She swallowed. Hard. Wanted to move *in* to his touch, and his warmth.

Which makes zero sense. I don't know this man.

He shifted her closer, and it dawned on her that the hardness she'd been aware of moments before was his chest—his very *muscled* chest from the feel of things, hidden under a baggy shirt.

Lila was plastered against him, her torso propped into his, but sideways, and she wanted to turn toward him, move nearer. If she did, it would put her breasts against his pecs. As good as that might feel, it wasn't something she should want to do to a stranger.

Something about the style of his garment tickled her mind, told Lila to take notice. The neckline had laces, and the sleeves billowed in the wind—like something she'd seen at the Renaissance Fest she'd attended a few times at home in Texas before she'd achieved her fellowship. He wore a kilt, too; the tartan pattern matched the one she was wrapped in.

Did he have a sword?

Yes, because the hilt shifted in and out of view as the horse plodded along.

Something's wrong.

"A'fore ye ask, nay, ye dinnae be dreamin'."

"Your shirt is ripped," she blurted. Lila had to forbid herself from sticking her fingers in the large hole on his shoulder to touch the flesh peeking out. A tiny scratch glared an angry red. The doctor in her wanted to tend it, even if it was little-kid-mild.

He arched a dark eyebrow, as if that was the last thing, he'd expected her to say.

It probably was. Her mouth had a hard time cooperating with her brain.

Why is everything so fuzzy?

His vivid eyes raked her face, and he frowned, but it didn't detract from his good looks. "Did ye hit yer head?"

Lila blinked.

Had she?

Thinking—remembering—*anything* took effort, and her head ached. "I…"

"What year are ye from, lass?" He lowered his voice.

Somehow, his volume made her feel better and had her heart skipping at the same time. Her eyes found his, but she frowned, too. "What an odd question."

His lips twitched. "Dinnae be really, but I understand why ye'd think so."

That just confused her more.

Lila let her gaze wander over the ground, not

going by in any kind of a hurry. The familiar landscape was the same from when she'd wandered down to the beach with Sophie and Lizzie—hilly and green—and seemed to go on for miles without even the hint of anything modern. Not a car or a paved road in sight.

That's odd, isn't it? Where's the bus?

She could hear the repetitive rush of water—waves rolling in—and smell the sea in the air, so the beach couldn't be far.

The beach—the Isle of Skye.

Was that where she was?

Where were her friends?

"Lass?"

Oh.

Right, she'd not answered him. Lila's temples throbbed and she rubbed her head.

"Yer really worryin' me." His brow was furrowed, like he really cared.

Why? He didn't know her.

"It usually dinnae take this long…"

Wait, what does that mean?

What doesn't take long?

Her mouth wouldn't form the words to speak the questions aloud.

She didn't fight him when he cupped her face and tilted up, so she'd have to meet his eyes again.

God, they were so blue.

Studying her as if looking for a real problem.

Lila's mind shouted a demand for him to stop touching her, but it was never born.

His fingers were gentle and warm, like the rest of his body against hers.

Somehow, even though it didn't—*couldn't*—make sense, she only wanted more. "Are you sure I'm not dreaming?"

He chuckled, and it too, was warm, dancing over her skin like a new touch. The vibration rumbled in his chest against her shoulder.

The man that didn't feel so much like a stranger anymore shook his head, and the slight smile that curved his lips still flipped her stomach. "Aye, I'm sure. But if I tol' ye why, ye'd dinnae believe me."

"Try me."

chapter three

ngus stared down into the dark brown eyes that had finally cleared of her confused haze. That should make him feel better — she wasn't damaged — but the set of her mouth made his gut quiver.

This lass wasn't anything to be trifled with.

Whoever she was, whatever year she was from, instinct told him she was used to getting her way. She was used to being in charge.

He didn't question how he could know such a thing. Part of his magic was visions, premonitions, and even though he hadn't had one concerning the stranger in his arms, something whispered his notions about her were as right as if the future had clearly been dropped into his lap.

In a matter of speaking, it had been.

Angus wanted to assure her he'd love to '*try*' her as she'd dared him — even though he'd understood the meaning of her odd phrase because of his aunt. He couldn't tear his gaze away, nor did he want to lie to her.

He took a breath. "Ye've traveled through time. 'Tis tha year a' our Lord, sixteen hundred ninety an' two. 'Tis why I asked *when* yer from, lass." He kept his voice as even and serious as he could, so she wouldn't think him mad.

She stared. Her delicate throat jumped as if she'd swallowed, and for some reason, he wanted to place his lips against it, feel her skin repeat the action.

He hollered at himself for nonsense, but the longer she remained silent, the more Angus wanted to shift on Magda's back, especially when his bollocks tingled with interest. He'd slowed the mare to a walk so he'd have an ample stretch to talk with the time traveler, prepare her for all she'd see; although they *should* hurry back so he could check on his da.

His troublesome kin weren't in sight—his sister had likely *blinked* herself and Liam back to the castle since they'd not taken mounts when they'd gone to the cave.

Angus, too, could travel telepathically, but he'd been agitated, and doing so required a calm mind. So, he'd opted for his horse when his mother had ordered him to continue after Lexi and Liam.

The lass cocked her head to one side, shifting that glorious length of dark locks, which brushed his wrist and his arm wrapped around her, tickling.

It was his turn to swallow. He ached—with want. Repeating that it made no sense didn't clear the lust clouding his brain, no matter how many times Angus tried.

"What?" she whispered.

He frowned, unable to decipher the word. He'd

expected her to reject his statement. It was only natural to disbelieve something like time traveling. From what his aunts had always said, there was no belief of magic in the century they'd traveled from.

Was this lass from the same time as his Aunt Claire and her sister, Jules? Or close to their time? From another era all together?

There was no known rhyme or reason about the Faery Stones' opening rifts in time. Just that those who'd come had been on the beaches of Skye in their century when they'd been sucked back.

Angus straightened and held her gaze. "When ye awoke this morn, what was the year?"

She blinked.

Ah, *now* she'd call him mad.

Her eyebrows drew tight.

He should ask her name, but he couldn't stop watching her changing expressions. She was appealing in every way he could imagine even as she struggled to process his words.

Dunvegan loomed, and soon she'd see the castle he'd always called home. The stronghold of his clan, the MacLeods, where his father was laird. Where he would be also, someday. He was nine and twenty, but his father was only one and fifty. Not an old man, despite the injury he'd sustained from the stallion's toss.

"It was…" She frowned again, and he wanted to trace the little bow of her lips with his tongue. "Did you say 1692?"

He nodded.

"Well, it sure as hell wasn't 1692." She tugged on his shirtsleeve. "*1692*? Are you sure you're not a reenactor?"

Angus cocked his head. "A re-what? Nay."

"It can't be the seventeenth century—" She seemed to notice the castle for the first time, and gasped, pointing a shaky finger at the embattlement where one of his clansmen stood watching their approach. "Dunvegan…but it looks…different."

Aunt Claire had told them their home had still been standing in her time, some three hundred and fifty years in the future, so he wasn't surprised to hear this lass mention much the same, even if he didn't know when she was from just yet.

"Aye, I'd imagine so."

"But…" She didn't say more, and her arm drifted back to her lap, as if she could no longer hold it aloft. Her head remained turned away from him, and he studied her pretty profile.

Her cheeks were still flushed with color, making her skin look creamy, tempting.

It took all Angus was made of not to lean down and kiss each one, then urge her face back toward him so he could take her mouth.

He wanted to comfort her, reassure her, but the gesture wouldn't be welcomed.

Would it?

Would she let him kiss her?

Stop. Now.

The inflection of her speech was also similar to his aunt and her sister, so he assumed she was also what they called, American. From a land far away, across the ocean. What was referred to as the New World or, the Colonies, by the stupid English in *his* time.

He'd known men, even whole families, that'd sailed there for a new life, and the distance was so great no one in Scotland was sure they'd be heard from again.

"Dinnae fash, things will make sense soon."

"Will they? You say I'm not dreaming. Your clothes aren't...normal, I'm on a horse, and this castle, which I saw earlier *today,* looks like it did in years past. From *history*. It's the seventeenth century, you said. When I woke up this morning, since you asked, it was the twenty-first. Oh, and I still don't have a freakin' clue why I'm naked."

Ah, so she is *from the same time as Aunt Claire and Jules.*

"The twenty-first? Then ye truly have no worries." Angus avoided the subject of nudity, as he didn't need a reminder that only his plaid separated him from her bare body.

Besides, details would come out later. He'd rather have his mother or aunt explain the Faery Stones. Maybe that way she'd have an easier time believing they—and magic—were real.

Her gorgeous dark eyes went wide, even as they reflected doubt. "Why's that?"

"My uncle's wife is from tha same time...yer century."

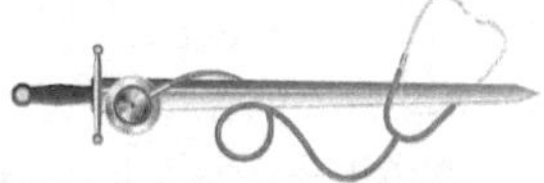

"What the hell?" and "You're crazy!" died on her tongue before she could say them.

Men shouted to each other as Lila held on to the stranger and the horse trotted into some kind of courtyard inside the massive gates around the castle she'd recognized as Dunvegan. The place she'd been supposed to tour with her friends.

That looked *nothing* like it had *that* afternoon.

There were embattlements, with men strolling about—on duty, not historical display. There was no flag, or antennas on top of it, either. Smoke wafted from chimneys. People in period clothing—seventeenth century evidently—milled about.

Lila's surroundings looked and felt authentic—to the year 1692, as he'd claimed.

Scents tickled her nose—not many of them pleasant, unlike the sandalwood fragrance of her...well, what was this man to her?

She swallowed—and not for the first time as her heart pattered harder. He'd said she wasn't dreaming, but...well, wouldn't someone tell her that *in* a dream?

Lila pinched her wrist. "Ow."

Her companion's lip rippled with amusement,

and his eyes danced.

Damn, he really did have fantastic peepers. So vividly sapphire.

"I tol' ye. Ye dinnae be dreamin'." He gestured to the scene before them. "'Tis all real."

"What if I can't accept that?"

He frowned. "Weel, I wish I could change things fer ye, but I dinnae be able ta."

Why did she have to find his brogue so alluring?

She matched his frown.

As long as she'd been in Scotland, Lila had never let how sexy a man *sounded* affect her. She hadn't taken a lover, and certainly wasn't about to…*in the freakin' past.* No matter how the sexiness extended to his person, not only his tone of voice or inflection.

He slid off the horse and she was cold without his body at her back.

She teetered and grabbed the mare's neck, but the blanket slipped off her shoulder and kept going, revealing her breasts. Lila tried not to shriek as she scrambled to re-cover herself, but when she looked at her companion, he was staring at her chest. Heat licked her neck and snaked into her cheeks, burning until she fidgeted.

"Sorry, lass. Shoulda warned ye."

"Ya think?" she snapped.

Remorse crossed his handsome face, but he lifted his arms. "Come. I'll take ye inside and get ye somethin' ta wear. An' somethin' ta eat, if ye so desire."

She tried not to shiver when his big hands encircled her waist, but she was more irritated at herself for the reason.

Lila wasn't cold.

She was *aware* of his touch. Anticipated it, even.

Her bare feet sank into mucky ground, but it didn't gross her out, even though it was cold; chilled her. She preferred to go without socks and shoes whenever possible, although over the years, many a colleague had accused her of its unsanitariness, and perhaps even danger.

Lila didn't need her feet for surgery, just her hands...and her brain. For a doctor, she'd never been a germophobe.

He still had her in his grip, and she should tell him to release her—she stood on her own, after all— but for the hundredth time since she'd woken in his arms, nothing came out of her mouth as she peered up at him.

The man was *tall*, probably had a foot on her five-five, and for some reason, she was tempted to slide her arms around him.

Handy that Lila had to clutch the plaid around her, of course.

He stared right back, and tremors danced down her spine.

He's definitely as hot as he sounds.

"Angus!"

They both jumped, and his hands slipped away.

She chided herself for missing his touch for the second time.

A diminutive woman lifted dark green skirts and hurried over. She appeared to be in her mid-to-late forties, but very pretty. Her long, blonde plait whipped behind her in her haste.

When the lady had closed the distance, Lila couldn't help but read the concern in her still-youthful expression, and it perked her curiosity.

Something's wrong.

Green eyes gave her a onceover, and Lila wanted to dart behind her companion—evidently, Angus—but she didn't.

"Who's this?"

He glanced at her. "I dinnae—"

"Lila." She cleared her throat when her name came out barely a croak. "Lila Salinas." She thrust her hand out to the blonde, then tucked it behind her back in a quick yank. Women in this century wouldn't shake hands, but she wasn't about to curtsey, given her…attire.

The woman cast her eyes to the sky, as if she hadn't noticed Lila's social faux pas. "They opened the Stones."

"Aye, they did."

She closed her eyes before sighing and meeting Lila's gaze. "I'm Claire. I apologize, but we don't have time to get properly acquainted." She looked at

Angus. "Your mother put your father to sleep with a spell, but the bone is sticking out of his leg. Malcolm needs help, but to do what I don't think even he knows. It can't be mended with a poultice, and it has to be set before he can be sewn up. He's lost a lot of blood. Xander and your mom said the wound is beyond what little healing powers they have. So, magic can't fix it."

The woman's accent wasn't Scottish. Well, sort of. Some words sounded off, like a combination of Scottish and…American?

Claire spoke fast, so Lila filed most of it away to examine later anyway, barely processing the words *spell* and *magic*. She discarded what didn't make sense, but latched on to what did. "Take me to whoever's injured."

Her command had both her companions stilling.

Two sets of eyes landed on her.

"My da fell off a horse," Angus said.

"Broke his leg," the woman said. "But it's bad—"

Lila nodded. "A compound fracture, by the sound of things. Do you know if it's the femur? Or the tibia? Fibula?" She gestured to her own leg as she recited the bones.

"It's lower leg. Sticking out of his shin," the older woman said.

So, not the femur. Good.

Hope lit Claire's green eyes. "You don't happen to be a—"

"Doctor. Yes. A surgeon, actually."

She put her hands together in a prayer gesture and thrust them high. "Oh, thank God! Come this way!"

chapter four

Rushing into the castle was a blur, and Lila would've liked to look around—she'd missed her tour after all—but there would likely be time for that later.

Claire tugged her hand, and she trailed the older woman up some stone stairs. The heavy footsteps behind them shouted her original companion followed.

"First, I'll grab you something to wear. You can't help naked…or wrapped in Angus' plaid."

"Well, I could, but I'm sure it'd turn some heads."

The woman offered a weak but genuine smile and glanced over her shoulder at Angus. "I like her."

Lila flushed and it took all she was made of not to look at the handsome man. Her rescuer, she supposed. She hated that her heart skipped because she wanted him to say *he* liked her, too.

That makes no sense, she repeated instead. *He doesn't know me* needed to become her new mantra.

"Come with me," Claire said, pulling her down a long dim hallway once they reached the top of the stairwell.

Angus broke off; entering a room to the right, but the older woman kept pulling Lila behind her—too fast to notice if that room contained the injured man. They went into another, three or four doors farther, and on the left.

"You look about my height, which is good." She bent over a trunk and dug inside.

"I'm five-five," Lila supplied, but the blonde didn't acknowledge her. Her eyes jogged around the room, taking in dark oversized furniture, all carved and beautiful, including the four-poster bed. An oak desk in the corner matched, and a rack of swords hung on the wall above it.

The single window was covered with heavy-looking drapery; only partially open, leaking a few slivers of light.

The only feminine touch in sight was light green bedding, but the comforter also had the same tartan pattern of the blanket wrapped around her. It was more like a quilt, with alternating blocks of green and plaid.

It was gorgeous, and she wanted to touch it. See if it was as fluffy as it appeared. The pillows looked inviting, and a part of Lila wanted to crawl on the bed and lay down.

She scolded herself—someone needed her; she could rest later.

A fire burned in the hearth, and she wanted to move toward it, warm her cold legs and feet, but they were pressed for time.

"*Mamaidh?*"

Lila's gaze shot to the ajar door.

A little boy with sandy hair stood halfway through the frame, obviously hesitant to step inside.

Claire shut the trunk, straightening with a blue dress in her hands. "Iain, what're you doing up here? Where are your brothers?"

He hung his shaggy head but came to the older woman when she gestured. "I wanna stay wit' ye..."

She sighed, tucked the garment under her arm, and then tipped his chin up.

He looked about ten or eleven, but he was almost as tall as his mother.

"Uncle Alex is gonna be fine. Find Lachlan and Rory. Stay with your brothers. Where're your cousins?"

"I dinnae ken about them, but Lan and Ror are in tha stables. I snuck away."

Claire pursed her lips, but she caressed the boy's cheek with obvious love. "I know it's hard and you want to help, but—"

"The best I can do 'tis stay outta tha way." The boy rolled his eyes and broke away from his mother.

Lila bit her bottom lip to keep from laughing. His pout was endearing, not irritating, and she'd not want to offend anyone.

The older woman tugged him back and kissed his forehead. "Aye, my love. Scoot. Tell your brothers not to fash. Shut the door on your way out." Claire shook her head when their eyes met. "My miracle baby. It's hard for him, since he's so much younger than the others."

"Oh?"

"Aye, Angus is the oldest child, and my Iain, named for his grandfather—God rest his soul—is the youngest MacLeod; he just turned ten. We lost my husband's da almost two years ago." Her mixed accent wrapped around the words, especially when she'd said, '*da*,' just like Angus had.

"I'd hardly call Angus a child," Lila blurted. Her cheeks heated, and she averted her gaze, clutching the tartan to her neck.

Claire laughed. "He'll always be my little nephew, even at almost thirty. He was barely Iain's age when I married Duncan. Like I said, he's the oldest of the kids, but the others are close in age. Angus and Iain are the outliers, poor things. But we can chat later; my brother-in-law really needs your help. Put this on." The woman thrust the blue material at her. "We'll have to find you some shoes later, hope that's okay."

"Fine, actually; I prefer bare feet." Lila let go of the blanket to catch the soft gown; nudity around another female didn't bother her as much as Angus staring at her naked breasts. She fought a shiver that had nothing to do with the room's temperature.

It didn't matter.

None of it mattered.

The body was the body, and as a doctor she'd seen it all.

She righted the dress and tugged it over her head. After smoothing the fabric down her front, she pulled the attached belt tight around her waist to secure it.

The garment fit well and was simple in design, with some light pink embroidery—flowers—at the neckline. Loose and comfortable. More importantly, the dress wouldn't impede her movements, and the sleeves were short, so they wouldn't get in the way during surgery, either.

"We'll get you a chemise and corset later, but we really need to get to Alex's rooms. Sorry, you do look like you'll need some support, and despite my efforts, there are no bras here. I can't really change history on purpose, though I do make linen panties. I'll get some of those for you, too."

Lila gasped. "You're the one…"

The woman cocked her head to one side, and her long braid danced. "One?"

"Angus said there was someone here from the twenty-first century."

Claire nodded and smiled. "One of two, actually. My sister, Jules, lives across the way. She married the MacDonald laird."

"How…how long have you been here?"

"Twenty years. Almost twenty-one."

Lila swallowed another gasp. "Twenty…"

"No worries, I wanted to stay. I met my husband. If you want to go home, I'm sure our magic can get you there. But first…"

She took a breath and gave a curt nod. That was the second mention of something that wasn't supposed to be real—*magic*. However, she could ask later. Lila had a patient. "Right. Take me to…Alex, you said?"

Claire nodded again and went for the door.

At least focusing on an injury—likely surgery—would help her worry less about all her unbelievable circumstances.

For now.

Someone would have to explain how magic was supposedly real when she was done fixing Angus' dad.

They entered a room that had similar furniture to the one she'd just left—Lila assumed was Claire and her husband's.

Too many people crowded around the bed, which she anticipated contained her patient. However, Angus wasn't among them.

Lila snapped into doctor-mode. Instinct ordered her to clear the room.

She might not know if she'd started to believe *when* she was despite her surroundings, but she was intimately familiar with what—*how*—she had to be as a physician.

For the first time since she'd woken in Angus' arms, she felt almost normal.

Lila straightened her shoulders and approached the bed, leaving Claire just inside the door. "I'm going to need everyone to step aside, please." She used the authoritative tone that never failed to calm, even as she was being obeyed.

Two fair heads—one male, one female—looked up first.

Then two dark ones, also one of each gender.

Another man, with bushy salt and pepper hair and spectacles resting on the end of his nose was the only one who didn't.

It appeared he was trying to staunch blood-flow. His hands were covered in the crimson mess—and blood spattered up to his elbows. The man's lack of gloves was another reminder she was far, far from home.

"Who are you?" The petite blonde woman whirled and perched bloody hands on the hips of her purple dress. She wore a splotched lilac apron—more evidence Lila needed to get to work—but made no efforts to wipe herself clean.

"Take a breath, cousin, she's here to help."

Lila's eyes landed on a fair-haired man standing behind her. Both had tresses lighter than Claire's. More platinum than blonde in hue. The woman's was long, wavy and free of constraint. The man's hair was shorter and shaggy like Claire's son, Iain's, had been.

"Relax, Alana, she's a doctor…from the future." Claire moved toward them. "Xander can read minds, but don't worry o'er him." She gestured to the man who'd spoken. "Y'all do what she says, and clear out.

Give her some room, let her look at Alex. She knows what she's doing."

Lila should thank the woman for having her back when she didn't know her, but she swallowed and approached the bed. She wasn't nervous about what she had to do; she was *freaked out* at where—and *when*—she had to do it.

Her patient was still and unconscious. Tall, like his son, with the same long sable locks, but he was going gray at the temples. Alex was probably in his early fifties, and just as handsome as Angus. Unlike his son, he wore a thick, groomed beard. It, too, was streaked with gray, but it made him appear refined, not aged.

He looked like he was in a peaceful slumber; however, his skin had a pallor she didn't like. He'd indeed lost too much blood.

They needed to control it, or they were going to lose him. Lila might not know Angus, but she sure as hell didn't want to see him watch his father die.

Especially not after the horrid week she'd had.

She'd lost a patient from something she shouldn't have—a sneak infection she should've seen coming. Something that was supposed to have been minor, only had ended deadly. Lila had taken it hard—part of the reason Lizzie and Sophie had whisked her off to the Highlands.

Reality was, doctors lost patients. *You can't save everyone* was something she'd heard often—and rejected every time.

Lila *would* save this man today. There were no other options.

If she had to pull off a transfusion 1692 style, she'd deal with it. Didn't want to guess at matching blood types, but again, if she had to, she would. She was O-negative, so she could be the donor and not harm her patient anyway.

"Malcolm, right?"

The man working on Alex's leg finally glanced at her with serious hazel eyes. "Aye, clan healer."

"Good. Keep doing what you're doing, but I need to see if the break was clean, or if the fracture splintered." If there were missing bone fragments, it could complicate things. She didn't want to contemplate that; just wanted to be sure and handle the problem.

Angus tumbled into the room with two buckets full of steaming water. How he managed not to slosh them all over was a wonder, but he set them by the hearth, and the dark-haired woman who'd been hovering over the patient's bed joined him.

"Fresh hot water is good, too," Lila murmured. She looked away from her rescuer, and her gaze collided with the blonde woman's. "You're his wife?"

She nodded. "Alana."

Her breath caught, even though she cautioned herself not to give into distraction. Her patient's wife's eyes were purple. Actual violet, and gorgeous, just like her face. She looked younger than Alex but was distinguished in a way that betrayed hidden years. "I know this is a scary situation, but it's going to be all right."

But is it?

Lila was in the late seventeenth century in a bedroom—albeit a big one. Space to work was the only thing on her side.

Nothing before her was sanitary, and the instruments the clan healer had bound to a thick strap of leather lying next to Alex's thigh on the bed were primitive at best.

The whole room was a germ.

An infection waiting to happen, even if she was able to set the bone, repair it—and any damaged muscle—before sealing him up. She could keep him from sepsis—*maybe* but couldn't be sure she wasn't sealing *in* infection.

Think, Lila.

What would her *lita* do?

As Claire had mentioned in the courtyard, a poultice couldn't fix it, but maybe some kind of herbs *could* help?

She could work *with* Malcolm instead of ultimately shoving him away after he'd finished with the bleeding. Holistic medicine had been around for thousands of years, after all.

Negative feelings—and loss—washed over her regarding natural remedies. Emotions she'd set in stone with every shouted word—in English and Spanish. Blame and guilt hit next, sharp and familiar.

Lila swallowed and pushed it all away. She couldn't dwell on that right now.

She had a man's life to save.

There was a leather satchel hanging half open on a nearby table that no doubt belonged to the clan healer, given the visible jars and dried plants. The man had to know more about his supplies than she ever could.

Whirling and taking a breath, she prayed she could channel Maria Santa Louisa Rodriguez Salinas.

Lita, *help me save this man. God, it wouldn't be bad to have You at my back, either.*

She smirked.

Her grandmother certainly would've admonished her for blasphemy and cautioned her to call for The Big Guy first.

The answer smacked into her forehead.

"Malcolm, do you have any yarrow?"

The healer pinned her with that hazel gaze and an arched, bushy eyebrow. "Aye, I'm usin' it, a' course. Bleedin' is much less than it 'twas."

Well, that's good and bad.

She needed to work fast. "I need to wash my hands." Lila glanced toward Angus and the buckets.

"Water's boilin', lass." Her rescuer had alarm in his voice.

"Good." She squatted at his feet, holding her

hands over the steaming buckets.

"Here's a clean cloth." The dark-haired woman who'd been by the bed thrust worn-looking linen into her hands. She resembled Angus enough to be his mother, but Lila assumed Alana was. Her eyes were the same blue as his.

"Soap. It's lye." Claire tossed a misshapen bar she barely caught.

Also good.

Lila got to the business of sanitizing as much as she could; while she did so, she quizzed Malcolm on what he'd done already.

The healer rattled off some herbs she recognized from her years of *Lita* trying to pound them and their uses into her head, as well as some she did not. He didn't seem to mind explaining, and she had to know what she was getting into, so she asked questions.

By the time she was at Alex's side with her fingers inside his leg, more people had come into the room, but Lila tuned them all out and got to work on the repair.

They maintained a respectful distance, so she didn't have to holler at anyone. She would've preferred them gone, but their presence wasn't defiling any kind of antiseptic, so she didn't see a reason to further worry a caring family. Would that all her patients had loved ones like Alex obviously did.

More good news; the break was clean, and even better; it was the smaller of the two lower leg bones, the fibula.

She fit the bone back together perfectly, but she had to stitch torn musculature, and of course, his skin where the bone had torn through his shin. "I need some thread. Sanitized, if possible."

Claire stepped forward when Malcolm said he had some in his bag and gestured toward the bedside table.

"He dinnae be my first patient, lass," the healer said. "I been healin' folks longer 'an ye've been alive, I'd suspicion."

Lila mumbled an apology and reminded herself not to assume he was a hick that didn't know what he was doing.

His training had just been different than hers.

Be respectful. This man is a colleague.

It was almost as if she could hear her grandmother's voice. Her neck heated even as she thanked Claire for handing the spool over.

"The thread is clean, I used whiskey," Malcolm said.

"Even better, thank you."

He nodded and assisted her in repairing the ripped flesh, and finally closing the wound.

"How long has he been out?" Lila asked over her shoulder. She recalled Claire mentioning that he'd been put to sleep with magic.

Perhaps it was as good as anesthesia?

It'd certainly been a comfort—to her, as well as

Alex—that he'd not had to endure the agony of being sewn up while awake.

Alana stepped forward. She wrung her hands on the apron she wore but didn't look as worried as she had when they'd rushed into the room, which was good. "Perhaps ten minutes before your arrival, the pain was too much."

"I'd imagine so." Lila worked out with Malcolm what he had for pain control and told Alex's wife she could wake her husband when she saw fit.

They'd already splinted the leg, and Lila went over some quick post-op care. She'd have to watch him like a hawk for infection. She refused to contemplate all the bad things that could happen.

The worst—amputation—haunted the back of her mind.

"Thank ye fer savin' my da!" A girl shoved away from Angus and rushed toward Lila, throwing her arms around her in a surprise hug.

She tried not to stiffen, and not just because she was covered in Alex's blood. She'd never liked to be considered a stereotypical hardass, barely-feeling surgeon, but she didn't often allow a patient's family to hug her.

The girl released her, and Lila met her violet eyes—just like Alana's. They were misty, and remorse darted across her young face. She couldn't be out of her teens, and if she was, it probably wasn't by much.

"This s'all my fault!" Tears coursed down her

cheeks.

Alana slid forward and pulled the girl close. "Alexandria, we will have words later, my love. Your father is out of danger now." She stroked the girl's long ebony locks and held her while she sobbed.

Lila swallowed and tried not to fidget. She didn't contradict the woman. Alex was still in danger of infection. Pointing it out would only upset the girl further, and possibly the rest of the family, even if it was true.

Her eyes collided with Angus' when she couldn't bear to look at the mother-daughter show of comfort anymore.

His chest heaved as if he'd taken a breath, and he mouthed "thank ye," as best she could guess.

For some reason, she wanted to go to him.

Claire cleared her throat and stepped away from the man who'd introduced himself as Duncan, Alex's twin brother, moments before.

She hadn't met all the MacLeods in the room, but nearly-grown children clung to adults, so Lila assumed they were grouped with their parents.

Iain stood in front of Duncan, and the man's large hands swallowed the boy's shoulders. Beside him was who she assumed were Claire's other sons, Lachlan, and Rory, if she remembered correctly. Both were dark-haired and almost as tall as their father.

"Lila-lass, let's get you cleaned up. I'm sure you're hungry," the older woman said.

She offered a nod and followed Angus' aunt from the room, but her eyes couldn't help but latch onto him until she couldn't see him anymore.

chapter five

a woman he didn't know—his family didn't know—had saved his father.

As he watched his mother hold his crying sister, Angus was torn. He wanted to follow Lila out of the room with Claire when he should *want* to remain with his family.

Lila.

Even her name was beautiful.

Gratefulness washed over him. Perhaps he should thank his pesky younger sibling and cousin for being reckless idiots.

The lass had come from the future when she was needed, and helped their father in a way Malcolm Beaton couldn't have on his own. Perhaps she was *supposed* to have come back to them today.

Was that too foolish a thought?

A voice whispered a word his mother often uttered—*fate.*

Can it be so?

Angus was so sucked into his own mind; he'd missed the healer cleaning up and clearing out of the rooms. His mother had also calmed Lexi's sobs.

His eyes rested on the closed door, and he tried to convince himself he wasn't begging it to open to reveal Lila.

She'd looked lovely in the borrowed blue dress, although he'd named himself a wretch for watching the shifting movements of her generous breasts beneath the fabric. She'd not worn a corset, and her feet remained bare.

His Uncle Xander—who was actually his cousin by blood, as well as the fated mate of his father's sister, Janet—rested his palm on the laird's forehead and murmured lowly in Fae.

The words weren't so different than Gaelic, but Angus didn't expend efforts to translate the spell.

His da started to come around, but then his face contorted, and he reached for his injured leg, as if on instinct.

"Alex, be still." His uncle's deep voice was calm, and his father obeyed, blinking a few times before he opened his eyes.

"Alex, love, all is well," his mother cooed, stroking his cheek.

"Da!" Lexi whined.

His father's eyes landed on his mother first, looking free of any magic, sleep, or pain-induced haze. "Alana?" His dark brows were drawn tight, as if confused.

His mother sat gingerly on the edge of the bed. His sister stood close enough that her knees touched her gown-clad thigh.

Angus should join them, but he stood a few feet

away, watching as if those before him were strangers.

"What do you remember?" his mother asked.

"Gettin' thrown from Dragh's back! Tha' ornery git dinnae be half tha stallion his sire was." His father threw some curses around that shouldn't be uttered in the presence of females and shook his head, making his deep brown hair dance. He then mourned the loss of his old stallion, Bán, who was his current mount's father.

The old horse had been dead for a year or so, and the laird was still working on taming his young replacement. Not well enough, as the day's incident attested. It was a diatribe Angus had heard often. His father had been very attached to the white stallion.

Alex's sharp gaze landed on Lexi. "Ye, lass, an' I, shall have words."

His sister whimpered and sucked her bottom lip into her mouth. She blushed, too, which was decent of her. "I'm so sorry, Da."

"Later, love." His mother reached for his father's hand, softening her reproach, and glanced over her shoulder at Angus.

He cleared his throat and joined his family at the bedside. "A lass came from the far future an' likely saved yer life, Da. Ye were bleedin' badly. She's a healer. So, no' all was bad about tha little fools managin' ta open tha Stones." He threw a glare at his sister, but Lexi averted her gaze and fidgeted.

"A skilled one, love. She calls herself a surgeon."

Alana's voice was even, calm. She patted her husband's forearm.

His father's brow knitted again as he examined his injury. His hand shook as it hovered over the splint, as if afraid to touch his own leg. "I feel like a fool myself. I dinnae be novice a' horseback."

"Ye dinnae be a fool, Da. I am," Lexi muttered, hanging her head.

"None of this is for now," their mother said, still in that soothing tone.

Angus sucked back a sigh.

The laird and his sister both seemed to calm; perhaps his mother had used her empathic magic, or maybe it was just her voice, but even he relaxed.

Alex was still examining his right leg. The wound was dressed and bound, but the swelling was still present. The neat line of sutures on the inches-long cut appeared strong, holding the angry flesh together.

Lila had said she'd keep an eye on it, and although she hadn't voiced worry, she'd looked concerned.

He'd have to demand why later. If a physician of her obvious skill was worried, they needed to know about what.

"Does it pain you, brother?" Xander asked.

"Aye, a bit." The laird's hair shifted again with his nod, drawing attention to his graying temples.

Angus snorted. It probably hurt like hell, but his father wouldn't admit that aloud, especially to another man.

"Malcolm said for you ta take this for pain." Alana pressed a cup to his lips. "Drink slowly, love, and 'twill help."

His father obeyed, and his parents' gazes locked when she cradled the wooden mug afterwards.

His mother's mouth quivered. "I thought...I—"

"Dinnae fash, *mò chridhe*. I'll be hale in no time." Alex stroked his wife's cheek, like she had his moments before.

Silence fell as the couple regarded each other.

Angus was suddenly envious of the display of love he'd seen between his parents all these years.

Why?

His father had always been openly affectionate of the woman who'd birthed him and his sister, and his mother even more so — toward all three of them.

Lila's smile darted into his thoughts, and he called himself every curse word he could think of — in Gaelic, Fae, *and* English.

He didn't know the lass he'd brought home, even if she had saved his father's life.

His uncle threw him a knowing look.

Stay out of my head. Angus shot the words at Xander mentally, and the look in the man's violet eyes told him the message had been received — even if he wasn't the least bit repentant.

Lexi had always had trouble speaking telepathically — as his Aunt Claire had named it — but

Angus and Alana could do so with ease, as could his former Fae Warrior uncle, Xander.

The man smirked and shook his head.

Angus chose to ignore him and glanced back at the rest of his family.

Lexi knelt by the bed, clinging to their father's hand, and spilling her side of things with hurried sentences. She was crying again, and he could feel her genuine remorse, even though his mother was the empathic one.

His sibling must indeed be sincere, because their mother caressed her back as she spoke, with none of her famous ire present.

The former princess had quite the temper, especially when Lexi was disobedient. They'd had their fair share of shouting matches that his father — or himself — calmed over the years. The older his sister grew, the more stubborn she'd become, and the more independence she'd demanded.

When she married, her husband was in for it. The man had better be strong-willed, or he would never win over her antics.

Angus snorted. It was hard to imagine his little pest married, even if she *was* old enough.

He growled. Never mind, he'd kill any man who tried to touch her.

Lila's face again danced into his thoughts. He wanted to run through any man who tried to touch *her*, too.

What's gotten into you?

He repeated the thing he'd been telling himself all day.

I don't know her.

His sudden possessiveness didn't change. Angus wanted to more than *possess* her. It didn't matter that he didn't know her. Perhaps it even went beyond the physical. He wanted to get to know her. Speak with her, make her laugh. Show his gratitude for her saving his father.

He shook himself when his uncle threw him another look, this time with a fair eyebrow arched. Angus mumbled a spellword that blocked his thoughts from Xander's magic.

It's not like I want to hear you. His uncle's voice appeared in his head, not his ears. *You're thinking loudly, as if you have a…new obsession.*

Angus chose not to answer. He also ignored Xander's following snort.

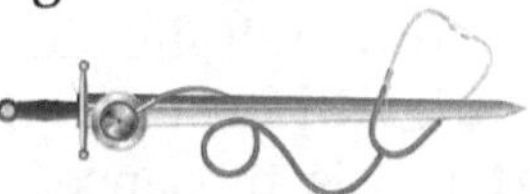

Malcolm's surgery, as he called it, was on the lowest level of Dunvegan, a sprawling, yet cozy room. It was dim, but that only added to the welcoming aura that washed over her, despite that it was so opposite from any healthcare-related room she'd ever stepped foot in. Hospitals, no matter US, or UK, had always been over-bright, stale lights everywhere.

Lila had never seen anything like what was

before her. Her *lita* would've been in heaven. The walls were lined with tables, and each surface held banks of tiny drawers, like mini clothing dressers, or old-school library catalogs. Just like the forgotten Dewey Decimal System, they were all labeled, bearing the name of the contents; a plethora of spices, herbs, and more things floral than she'd imagined. She never expected the sheer amount could have medicinal properties.

Should've listened to Lita *better.*

The old ache, and the even older argument, echoed in her head and heart. Only, being dead-set on holistics hadn't saved her grandmother from cancer, and it never could have, no matter the old woman's insistence. However, she could've respected *Lita's* beliefs a bit better—Lila still chided herself for that almost daily. It was too late to apologize.

Malcolm wasn't old enough to be her grandfather—perhaps her father, as he appeared to be in his early sixties. Although she didn't know him, she felt the kindred spirit within her reaching toward him. She took comfort in his presence, despite her dark memories.

Maybe it was this huge room, his obvious knowledge of something her grandmother had sworn by, or even that he was a colleague of sorts.

Lila couldn't put her finger on it, but she was drawn to him, this doctor of 1692. Perhaps she could learn from him—learn things to take home to the future. It would definitely make her *lita* proud.

The knowledge wouldn't heal the perpetual agony of losing her—she doubted anything would—but perhaps could help her soften the blow of sharp recollections of arguments that hadn't had answers she'd agreed with, and the guilt still haunting her.

Lila was still convinced if her grandmother hadn't been so stubborn, she could've lived longer, that a surgical approach *would've* helped, even though not all her doctors had agreed.

Her grandmother's faith hadn't saved her, any more than her herbs and spices.

When she'd lost her *lita*, she'd buried any faith she'd held. The answers were supposed to be in science.

Lila fought the sudden urge to close her eyes when her grandmother's voice washed over her, an admonition so familiar, she'd almost welcome it if she could hear it once more in her real life thick Spanish accent.

'You must have faith, mija, or what else do you have?'
I don't have you, for sure.

She'd lost her parents, too, but she'd been too little to remember them. Her grandmother had been her world.

Malcolm was speaking, but she had trouble clearing her thoughts to focus on the brogue that was slightly different—but no less appealing—than Angus'.

The man had told her he wasn't of the Highlands originally but had been living with Clan MacLeod since he'd been a young healer, first employed to save the former laird's wife. His hazel eyes had been sad when he'd confessed, she had suffered from consumption, and he'd been unable to cure her.

Lila had told him TB was still around in her time, with medicine-resistant strains, but he didn't look comforted. She glanced at a friendly fire, lit in the larger of two hearths. The blaze warmed the room, and somehow made her feel a little better.

In the very least, she'd done something good today. She'd helped Malcolm save his laird.

Angus' father.

She hadn't had to see her rescuer lose the man because of something like blood loss. Hopefully, she could keep him from infection, so he would have a full recovery.

Behind a curtain in the corner, Lila spotted the end of a cot or small bed. So, it seemed as if the healer lived where he worked.

The room smelled good, something she couldn't identify. Perhaps the different spices and herbs offered a mixed fragrance that was pleasant instead of overwhelming.

"I've prepared a poultice for the swelling," Malcolm said after they'd cleaned up and sat comfortably in his domain.

"What's in it?" Lila asked as she explored his vast

collections. She opened a few drawers and inhaled, closing her eyes when something appealed, like lavender.

She kept her dark emotions regarding her loss on the fringes, enough to enjoy her unusual surroundings.

The healer let her examine his things without comment as he rattled off what he'd placed in the remedy for the laird.

"Hmmm, I really wish you had some turmeric." She traced her lips, thinking about Malcolm's Scottish answer. "The yarrow will help, but turmeric is better."

"This poultice 'twill take down the swellin' well enough," he insisted softly.

There was a knock at the door, and Claire slipped into the large room. "Thought I'd find you down here, Lila." She had a basket full of what looked like fabric. "I've got a few underthings for you and a corset."

"Oh, thanks."

"I shall return ta tha laird." The healer stood from his stool near the hearth.

Lila sighed but flashed a smile for the older man. "Well, it's not like we can run to the pharmacy, so I suppose that'll have to do."

His face twisted in confusion, and Claire laughed.

"She means the apothecary, Mal."

"Oh, sorry." Lila cringed. "Well, erm…if you ever encounter an…apothecary from India or Asia, get some turmeric. It should be a yellow powder if it's already refined."

He offered her a curt nod and disappeared.

"C'mon, let's go back upstairs," Claire said. "We need a room with a looking glass."

The older woman had done as promised and outfitted Lila properly—seventeenth century style.

She now wore a corset and ladies' slippers, as well as a chemise under the borrowed dress, which had been cleaned after Alex's surgery. Plus, some basic panties beneath the gown.

The bodice was simple and ivory, fitted around her waist and over her chest on the blue gown in a way as to not obscure the flower embroidery at the neckline.

A mirror revealed Lila looked nice, but the outfit still felt more like a costume.

Her wonder hadn't settled about the unbelievable circumstances, but at least she could somewhat breathe. Claire hadn't tightened the laces at her back too much, yet her breasts were supported.

She surveyed her work with a smile. "Lookin' good."

Lila took another perusal, but when she met the woman's green eyes, she returned her smile. "Thank you. Too bad all this is real, and I'm not just dressing for the Renn Fest."

Her companion laughed. "I had a very similar thought the first time my sister-in-law, Janet, dressed me when I came here all those years ago. You'll do fine here."

You'll do fine here and *all those years ago* reverberated, so she wasn't sure how to answer. Lila's instinct was to assure Claire she wasn't staying, but she was…for a while. At least until Alex was on his feet.

"I can't believe the day got away from us, but dinner will be served soon. We should head down ta the great hall. I'm sure Angus is anxious ta see you."

Lila startled, but kept her mouth shut, and she merely forced a nod.

chapter six

ila sighed and let her eyes trace every piece of furniture in the guest room she'd been shown to. She stood in the center, as if she couldn't take steps forward or back. The bed was huge and seemed to dominate the place, and the hearth was lit with a crackling fire. A trunk at the end of it held more blankets, and a wash bin stood on a bedside table. The comforter was a MacLeod tartan quilt, and she wanted to test its fluffiness.

She'd been fed, bathed, and wore a soft sleeping gown Janet, her patient's sister, had given her. The pretty older woman was the one who'd handed her the cloth to wash her hands before Alex's surgery. She was Angus' aunt, and she'd helped her undress like Claire had helped her dress before supper.

Night had fallen, and Lila should be exhausted. She replayed the day in her head, from the moment she'd woken against Angus' warm bulk to the impromptu surgery.

She'd checked on her patient before Janet had shown her to this room. It was small in comparison to Alex's, but she didn't mind.

Her patient was too much like his son. Sitting at

his bedside and peering at him was like looking into Angus' eyes.

Alex had been charming, and grateful. Their conversation hadn't wholly consisted of his health and the wound. He'd asked questions about Lila—from where and when she'd come. He'd made the effort to get to know her.

Instinct told her he was a good man, so if she had to get lost in time, it was relief ending up in the care of a family like the MacLeods.

It could've been so much worse; but not only did they believe *when* she was from, they had two women from the twenty-first century there, and from Texas to boot. She hadn't met Claire's sister, but it blew her mind that they were from her home state.

They'd actually be around her age of thirty as well, had they not come back in time and stayed where twenty years or so had elapsed.

Lila shook her head. She couldn't wrap her mind around the whirlwind day, so she needed to release all things complicated for the night. Magic being *real* also led the charge on what she needed to put to bed.

Although, she wished she'd known something about Clan MacLeod. Done some reading beyond the tourist brochure she and her friends had received on the bus.

Would it matter?

Probably not.

Alana had assured her she could get back to the

future when she wished, but Lila wasn't going anywhere until Alex was healed. Or at least, able to stand.

That could be weeks, but she'd have to make sure his wound was healthy daily, and she couldn't let her focus slip.

The sutures had looked promising this evening, and the laird was sleepy from Malcolm's pain draught, but it was better that he rested anyway. She'd told the healer he could apply his poultice for the swelling and so far, it seemed to be working well.

Lila was surprised and pleased; her *lita* would've been proud that she'd learned something new related to holistic meds. She'd had to admit the healer had had the right of things. The idea didn't have as much bite as she'd assumed it would.

She could see her grandmother in her head, wearing the smug smile she'd always sported when she was correct.

The woman had been stubborn. Which Lila had inherited, as well.

Lila sighed when other memories followed. When her *lita's* smugness about natural ways hadn't been welcome, and the oncologist's order had been ignored, but she tried to shake the thoughts away. Didn't need anything to dim the positives for Alex.

Bad memories wouldn't change a thing.

Once he'd fallen asleep, the laird's wife had worried he'd be restless when he learned he'd be confined to a bed and would likely do something stupid.

Lila had assured Alana she'd help as much as she could, and Angus had joked his mother could keep his father asleep with magic.

The laird's wife had agreed she might have to.

Lila smirked. Men weren't always the best patients, especially the alpha-type she suspected Alex was, but the laird had never met *her* before.

Hopefully, she wouldn't have to unleash her temper on the man. *Lita* had also gifted her with that, although Lila was able to control herself better as an adult than when she was a kid.

They'd sure had some shouting matches over the years, even when her grandmother had gotten sick. Especially then, because the woman hadn't agreed with Lila's care-plan.

The knock on the door was soft, and instinct told her who it was.

Her focus scattered—but maybe that was a good thing. Her stomach jumped even as she whirled to face the carved wooden panel, and told Angus to come in.

He gave her a onceover that had her heart skipping, but he didn't say anything, or step further into the room until their eyes met.

"Angus? Do you need something?"

Somehow, his eyes darkened, but he blinked, and Lila doubted the intensity she must have imagined.

"You can come in here, you know, I won't bite you." She tried to convince herself to relax, but her pulse was far from normal.

Why?

Her rescuer cleared his throat and took a few steps toward her. He was dressed like she'd seen him earlier, in a kilt with a loose ivory shirt tucked in, and a thick belt around his trim waist, but this one wasn't ripped. His hair was wet. He'd bathed and smelled of fresh sandalwood and sage.

The mixed aroma washed over her and tickled her senses. As tempting as he was.

The door stood ajar a few inches, and Lila looked from that small gap, and back to Angus' face. His jaw sported a tempting shadow, and she tucked her hand behind her back when her fingers itched to trace each chiseled line.

She could almost feel the coarseness under her fingertips.

What is wrong with you?

"Ah, lass. I have somethin' I think belongs ta ye."

"What?"

His fingers disappeared into the leather pouch dangling from his belt. He held something up seconds later.

"My necklace!" Her hand went to her neck, which was silly, considering her rescuer had the white gold chain in his large grip. Lila rushed over and snatched the broken jewelry. She held it tight and pressed it over her heart.

"'Tis meanin'ful ta ye, I see."

"Yes, thank you so much. It was a gift from my grandmother. With everything that happened, I didn't even realize it was gone." Lila threw her arms around Angus in a hug.

They both froze, and their gazes locked.

What was she doing?

Since when are you the hugging type?

She swallowed and told her arms to drop to her sides, but they didn't. His heat sank into her through the thin gown, reminding her the barrier to her nudity wasn't much.

Angus didn't wrap her in his arms, but that didn't keep her from feeling his muscled torso against her upper body — or remember what it was like to be in his secure embrace.

When Lila's nipples tingled, she hollered at herself to move away. "I'm sorry." The blurt fell from her lips and she had to avert her eyes. Warmth rushed her cheeks, and she hoped like hell the room was dim enough for him to not notice.

The sound of him clearing his throat a second time drew her gaze back to his handsome face.

"Dinnae fash," Angus said.

"Thank you for returning my necklace, even if it's broken." Lila needed a distraction. "Your father's doing well."

"I came from seein' him. He sleeps. Thank ye,

lass, fer what ye did. I dinnae get a chance ta say it a' fore."

"It's my job." The standard answer fell from her lips, but her heart sped up all over again.

Why was the truth making her a nervous wreck?

"Weel, no matter. I'm grateful. My da…he holds my clan, my family…tagether." Admiration for the man shone from Angus' sapphire eyes, so she didn't contradict him.

In her estimation—granted it'd only been one day—his mother was the family glue. Alana was fiercein her love for Alex and their daughter, and she didn't doubt the woman felt the same about the man before Lila.

She'd been told that Lexi, Angus' little sister, as well as one of his cousins, Liam, were responsible for bringing her back in time, and even though she didn't understand the magic of it, it'd been an accident. Both young people were in quite a bit of trouble over *it and* hadn't been in the great hall for dinner.

The idea that they'd *needed* her for the laird's injury tickled the back of her mind. Her *lita* always said everything happened for a reason.

Lila cleared her throat like he had. "Thanks are unnecessary, but you're welcome. Alex will be fine, given time."

"Will he walk…again?" Hesitation coated the words, and she wanted to reach for him again.

She managed to keep her hands to herself. Barely.

"Yes, I don't see why not. At worst, he'll have a limp, but I was able to knit the bone seamlessly, so he may not. He just needs to stay off of it as he heals."

Angus released an audible breath. "I dinnae ken how ta thank ye."

"Angus, seriously, it's not—" Lila's breath stalled when he cupped her cheeks. Her mind screamed for her to pull away, but she stood as if transfixed, and stared up into his eyes.

So blue.

He dipped down as if he'd kiss her—but only for a moment. His touch fell away and he took a step back. His chest heaved as if he'd sucked in a breath, and hers echoed its obvious shakiness.

She needed him to leave. Before Lila did something stupid.

Had she imagined his intent?

Was he really about to kiss me?

What would she have done if he *had* kissed her?

If he tried again?

She left the questions dangling in her head because her instinctual answer was *completely* unacceptable.

Lila wouldn't—*couldn't*—kiss a man she didn't know, even if he made the first move. If he *had* actually kissed her, she should've—would've—shoved him away.

Right?

She blinked, and when she refocused on him,

Angus was even further away—millimeters from the door.

"Ah, I'll bid ye good night, lass."

"Oh, okay."

Loca, *don't you want him to leave?*

Angus retreated and closed the door silently.

She stood there, staring and calling herself every name she could think of when disappointment—and perhaps a little hurt—hit in her in waves she promptly ignored.

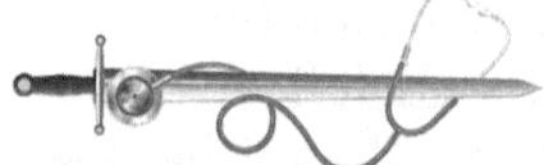

Angus paced his room. He'd almost *kissed* her. He swallowed when his cock jumped, then he squeezed his eyes shut.

Why was he having such a strong reaction to her?

He'd never experienced anything like this with any other lass, and he'd had lovers. Not the vast collection his Uncle Duncan had had before he'd married, but Angus had been with his fair share of women.

Xander had always told him when he'd finally found the one, he was supposed to be with, none of the others would cross his mind.

His father's twin only had eyes for his wife from the far future, so it appeared he shared Xander's wisdom.

According to his mother, there was *one* out there, designed specifically for him. She believed with all her heart his father had always been her fate, and her children were no different.

Angus had never met his grandmother, but his grandfather had wistfully mused about his wife many times over the years, and the day the old man had died, he'd told his family he was at peace; he was about to rejoin the love of his life.

"Love of his life?" Angus took another turn in his room and tasted the words.

All the couples around him, his parents included, had referred to their partner as such. Aloud. In his presence at one or more times — always.

Did he want the same?

What the *hell* was he even thinking?

Wanting a woman didn't mean anything beyond the physical. Rutting. Swiving, tupping, wenching. He'd heard it called many things. Aunt Claire simply said sex.

He wanted Lila, aye.

There was nothing more to it.

The knock on his door made him jump. It opened without invitation.

"Angus?" His mother closed the door quietly behind her. She took one look at him and wore a deep frown. It marred her beauty.

"*Màthair*? What's wrong?"

She crossed the distance to him, her purple gown swishing as she sauntered. Alana took his hands. She looked up at him, her violet eyes keen. "I was going to ask you the same, love."

"Why?"

"I could feel your torment from the other room. What troubles you?"

Angus sighed and cursed empathic magic to hell and back. Or to all five levels of Fae hell, an epithet his Uncle Xander often invoked. "Nothin', Ma."

Disbelief darted across her timeless face, and she arched a fair eyebrow. As full-blooded Fae, his mother appeared much younger than her seventy odd years.

Alana looked no older than his father and Duncan, who were one and fifty. Her countenance was ethereal, especially with her purple eyes. No one but family knew for sure she wasn't human, although there were whispers all over Skye.

"Angus MacLeod, are you lying to your mother?"

He smirked. "Wit' little success."

The former princess smiled and squeezed his hands. "My son, you've always told me when something bothers you, why stop now?" She tugged on his fingers and led them to his bed.

He sighed as they sat on the edge, and he shook his head.

"Is it your father? Lila, Goddess bless her, saved him. He'll be fine."

Angus tried not to startle at her name, but *of course*, his perceptive mother noticed even the barest fidget. No matter how minute, she always did. Something his sister complained about constantly.

Their mother had been the one to discover Lexi and Liam's intent for the Faery Stones, but only after they'd left Dunvegan. If it'd been ten minutes before, they might've caught the young fools.

His father wouldn't have been thrown from the horse, and Lila...

The physician wouldn't be in a guest room down the hall.

We never would've met.

"You think of the lass," his mother whispered, but he didn't like the matter-of-fact edge.

"I thought only Xander could read minds." He kept his voice dry, but knowing her, she wouldn't care.

Alana smiled, confirming his suspicion. "Aye, but I know my oldest bairn well." Her expression was fond, and she stroked his stubbled cheek.

He didn't bother chiding his mother for calling him a bairn. He hadn't been a child, let alone a baby in years. "Ye always say everythin' happens fer a reason, aye?"

She nodded.

"What if..."

"I thought the same thing this afternoon. Lila came back to us because she was needed."

Angus looked up at the ceiling of his quarters. It was so quiet the crackle of dying embers in his fireplace sounded overpowering. "I found her."

"Aye."

He met his mother's eyes at the simple answer, and she wore a soft smile. He didn't speak.

"You feel…a certain draw to her."

Angus wasn't surprised, nor did he want to try a denial she wouldn't believe anyway, so he merely nodded.

Her smile widened. "Perhaps the lass is your fate, as your father is mine."

"She's from tha future."

Alana laughed, the low sound caressing. "Aye, love. As is Claire, and she is your uncle's fate. The same is true of her sister, for the Laird MacDonald. Could it not be possible for you, as well? You're nearly thirty, and not a lass in sight has drawn you like I suspect our new healer does. I worry about you."

"*Màthair*." Angus sighed the Gaelic address.

She shook her head, making her long flaxen locks shift around her like an aura. "Fate, my love. 'Tis real."

He didn't disagree, she would just reiterate. "She wants ta go back. When Da is better."

"As did your Aunt Claire, at one time."

"'Tis different."

"How so? 'Tis the same. She will change her mind. *You* will change her mind." Alana stood, and gave another gentle smile. "You will see, my stubborn child."

"*I'm* no' yer stubborn child." He thumbed his chest, flashing a mischievous grin.

"In this moment, you are. A trait I fear you and your sister received from your MacLeod side."

Angus chuckled. "Right, because my mother

dinnae be stubborn a 'tall."

Alana's impish grin took years off her face and was all the answer he got. She slipped from his rooms with only a telepathic, *Goodnight, love.*

Somehow his mother's voice in his head was a comfort, but it didn't calm Angus' whirling thoughts.

chapter seven

e heard the melody of their combined voices before he put his palm on the ajar door. Angus paused, but the sounds washed over him again anyway.

The clan healer said something, then Lila answered.

Then…laughter.

She was *laughing* with Malcolm Beaton?

Nay, that couldn't be true. The old coot couldn't charm a lass, could he?

He'd never married, and the whole clan had long speculated the reasons.

The healer had lived with them since before Angus' birth. As a young man, Malcolm had been charged with saving a grandmother Angus hadn't gotten the chance to meet.

His father's mother had suffered from consumption, and it'd been too late for her, but all his life his grandfather had told him stories of her. His father, aunt, and uncle, too. They'd said Lady Caitriona tended to be a gentle, quiet sort. She would've adored him; they all had assured him over the years.

Quiet. Gentle.

Two traits Angus didn't associate with his little healer...

Mine?

The laughter sounded again, as if Malcolm was some sort of genius jester.

He growled.

Absolutely, she was *his*.

Angus rushed into the healer's sanctum, greeting an obviously interruption-induced silence, and four wide eyes aimed at him.

No one said anything, and Malcolm arched a bushy eyebrow, shoving his spectacles farther up his nose. "Can I...help ye wit' somethin', lad?"

Angus' gaze locked onto the healer's hazel eyes, but only for a few seconds while he forced a headshake. He looked back at his object of desire — the lass he'd just claimed in his mind.

Lila looked lovely, as always, with her long ebony locks free and flowing, like a smooth curtain he wanted to caress. She wore the blue dress and ivory corset like the day she'd arrived — it must've been laundered, because the day before she'd worn a more modest green gown. The pink flowered embroidery framed her cleavage perfectly around the top of her bodice. Bringing her breasts to attention to any man who cared to look.

Angus wanted to slay them all.

Lila held a small basket of healing supplies — full

of fresh bandages and some dried herbs — as if she was about to exit the surgery. She still didn't speak, and her expression was full of skepticism pointed in his direction. She appeared to take a breath and opened her mouth. "Angus?"

He loved his name on her lips, even if her accent reminded him of his aunt from the far future. The physician's voice was thicker, huskier than Claire's.

His aunt's words had never snagged him — naturally — but every word Lila uttered ensnared Angus more, no matter how many she chose to speak.

They continued to stare at him.

As if he'd gone mad.

Angus cleared his throat. "Ah…I was lookin' fer ye, Lila." He made himself leave his gaze on hers, instead of traversing her body again, like he wanted.

"I was just headed to check on your dad."

"Good, good."

Malcolm smirked in his periphery, and Angus wanted to bark at him, but thought better of it. No need to *show* they'd unnerved him.

Had they?

He didn't want to admit it, even to himself.

Angus shifted his feet like a lad caught watching lasses undress and fought the urge to clear his throat again.

"I'll see you later, Mal. I'll check your poultice and apply the new one, if needed." Lila lifted the basket, pointing out the contents. "I want to make sure it's working and check those stitches. We need to keep them dry."

"Aye, lassie, sounds well and good."

Mal?

Lila was referring to the healer with such informality, as if she'd known the man all her life—like *he* had.

Jealousy swirled in Angus' gut, low and hot. He swallowed and listened to them exchange a few more words.

She sashayed past him without acknowledging him.

Despite the insult, his feet turned of their own accord to follow. He didn't bid Malcolm farewell, and ignored the man's low chuckle as they neared the door.

"Angus, what do you *really* want?" she asked without sparing him a glance.

Angus shut the surgery door and followed her into the corridor, watching the blue gown sway around her feet with each step.

You.

Her pretty eyes widened as she whirled on him, and he cursed himself.

He must've spoken aloud.

Lila's dark hair flew with her movements, blanketing her shoulders and cupping her face. She didn't say anything, but her lips parted as if she intended to speak, and her little pink tongue traced her plump bottom lip.

Angus sucked back a groan. He took two steps toward her as if answering orders. He crowded her, pinning her against the wall outside the surgery. Didn't give her time to protest or push him away; he dipped down and took her mouth.

Her basket hit the stone floor with a *thud*.

His first taste exploded on a moan—from Lila, not him. She didn't put her arms around him, but he'd take what he could get for now.

He begged entrance into her mouth, and with a tentative touch of her tongue to his, she let him in, strengthening mutual exploration as she slanted her mouth closer under his.

Lila was so sweet, so good—like Angus had imagined dozens of times, especially the previous night in his vivid dreams.

His memory had no issue recalling every inch of her nude frame on the beach, and his wicked mind had put those images to work—ten times over, in his bed, with his hands and mouth *all* over her.

Her body was soft, pliant against his, and the press of her breasts into him made him granite beneath his plaid.

Angus wanted to pull her away from the wall, hold her. Swing her up into his arms and run up the stairs. To his room or hers, it mattered not, as long as *this* continued, and he could take her.

Lila's hands wiggled between them, settling on

his pectoral muscles. When she tried to break the kiss, he leaned in more, deepening it instead. She whimpered and submitted, rubbing her tongue against his again.

A small push distracted Angus from getting further lost in *her* and the movements of their mouths. Then another, until he pulled back, and their eyes met.

"No, Angus." Her hands were rough on his chest, and Lila shoved him.

He had to take a step back to keep from falling. Surprise had him retreating, releasing her—but he regretted it as soon as their bodies no longer touched. He was so hard, he ached.

Lila frowned and tucked flyaway strands of hair behind one ear. She didn't look at him right away, but when she did, he had to suck back another groan.

Her creamy bronze skin flushed pink to her ears, and her lips were swollen. Her chest heaved as if she couldn't breathe normally, her breasts playing peek-a-boo in her corset, and that certainly didn't help clear his passionate haze.

"No, Angus," she repeated. "You...*can't* do that. *I* can't do that. It's not right."

Not right? What?

"Nay?" Angus' question was a hoarse whisper.

What was she denying?

She'd kissed him back with such hunger, giving herself over to him, tasting him as much as he had her, but he didn't have the right to kiss her?

Is that what she meant?

"I…can't. I need to check on your father."

His brain and mouth remained constrained under some sort of desire-disconnect, so he couldn't muster an answer or voice the questions flirting on the edges of his mind.

"I don't want you like that," Lila whispered, and she bent to retrieve her basket. Her hair flew up like a cape as she whirled away and sprinted down the wide hallway, creating distance between them as efficiently as she'd stitched his da's leg.

He caught something that sounded like, "I'm not here for that," before she disappeared around the corner. Angus should've been stunned. Instead, he wanted to call after her, accuse her of lying.

Her heart raced her feet as Lila hurried away from him in the dim corridor. She took the first case of stairs two at a time, until her chest burned, and she had to stop to breathe.

She plastered her back to the cool stone wall and tried to convince her iron grip on the basket's handle to loosen. Her palm smarted, so she switched sides and shook it.

"Damn," Lila whispered, looking over the deep grooves from where the woven wood had pinched. The skin wasn't broken, but the throb worsened.

She set the basket down to rub the spot, but it

didn't help. Nor was she really all that concerned about her not-quite-injury.

Angus had *kissed* her.

Worse, I kissed him back.

It'd taken everything Lila was made of to keep from wrapping her arms around him and burrowing into that hard chest. She'd kept her hands in front of her — until she'd mustered the ability to shove him away.

He'd looked — so *shocked*. His blue eyes had been wide, despite the darker hue of arousal also present in his stare. The surprise had ruined the tempting ruddy flush to his cheeks and the bright red, plump effect his mouth had gained from hers.

She'd allowed him to kiss her, but she'd been right there with him, pressing into his mouth, tasting him until her toes curled. It hadn't lasted long, but long enough to wind Lila tight.

Not long enough, a voice whispered.

Even now the pulsing between her thighs hadn't eased. She was antsy; wanted to pace.

Her blood heated in a way a mere kiss had never been done before. In short, she wanted to go back down the stairwell and jump Angus' bones.

Well, one in particular.

She'd felt his arousal against her. So, he'd been just as hot as her.

From one kiss?

Aye, to steal Angus' word.

Lila shivered, but she sure as hell wasn't cold. She rubbed her arm and took a few calming breaths, but her belly still quivered, and heat radiated from low in her gut.

She'd never had such a…hypnotic reaction to a man.

Her body wanted him.

No.

Deny it as she was—and would continue to do so—her breasts were heavy, her nipples tingly and her sex throbbing.

Lila couldn't sleep with a stranger—let alone a man from 1692—so her body would have to deal with the unrequited want. Her head wouldn't allow her to give in, no matter the draw. Besides, a kiss didn't mean…much, right?

Angus had kissed her, he hadn't declared…

"But he did." *That* was what'd had her turning to him.

She straightened and swallowed.

He'd *said* he wanted her.

Lila's heart—which had finally calmed from her run—skipped and sped back into overdrive. She'd *told* him she didn't want him.

Liar liar.

"Lila? Are ye weel, lass?"

A shriek slipped from her mouth, and she slapped a hand to cover it. Lila jumped away from the wall and knocked the basket over with her foot.

"Ah, I dinnae mean ta scare ye."

She looked up and met blue eyes—just like Angus'.

Damn the MacLeod blue eyes.

This man matched her patient to a tee, but since he was walking around with no splint or sutures, she was staring up at Duncan, not Alex. The laird wasn't physically capable at the moment, anyway. Duncan stood on the landing above her, making his impressive height more evident.

Tall was another appealing MacLeod trait.

Double dammit.

"Lass?" the older man said.

"Umm, it's okay. I'm…fine." Lila's heart tripped again, calling her a liar.

Concern drew his brows tighter, but he didn't speak. Those incredible eyes raked her face, like he was taking in every millimeter.

She wanted to rub her cheeks or smooth her hair. Angus had run his fingers through it. Was it obvious what she'd done moments before?

Her gut tightened, and she wanted to melt into the stone behind her.

To detract attention from her, Lila bent over and righted the basket, adjusting the contents as she returned the small jar of yarrow back inside. It'd been the only item that'd fallen out—which was good, considering she needed to keep the bandages clean, and didn't want the new poultice Malcolm had prepared to get damaged or dirty. "Is there something I can do for you?" she asked.

Duncan wasn't often seen in the lower levels of the castle — at least, Lila had never run into him in the days she'd been there.

The man descended the few steps between them and ran his hands through his long dark hair, as if nervous. His temples were graying like his brother, but Angus looked like him, as Alex did.

Different from the laird, his twin wore no beard, which made the resemblance more startling. There was no surprise what her rescuer would look like when he reached their age.

Somehow, it didn't matter…the man before her was just as good-looking as his nephew.

Thoughts like that were a waste — Lila would be back in the twenty-first century long before then, so she'd never see Angus age gracefully, or otherwise.

"'Tis, true, I was lookin' fer ye, lass." Duncan fidgeted and averted his gaze.

"Is something wrong?"

His eyes swung back to hers. "I was hopin' there dinnae be."

"What d'you mean?"

Angus' uncle frowned. "Is everythin' weel wit' my brother?" His worry was a live thing she could feel, and her instinct was to reassure him.

Lila squeezed his hand. His fingers were large and calloused, but warm. "Alex will be fine, but it'll be a while before he's back on his feet…fully healed."

His relief was apparent, and his massive chest heaved. For an older man, Duncan was still full of muscle, obvious even through a baggy shirt—called a leine, Claire had explained.

Lila frowned. "Did something happen to make you worry?"

"Nay. He's…'tis just…"

"Just what?"

"The pain is great. My brother tries ta hide it, a' course, but even three days later…" He cleared his throat. "'Tis concernin'."

She sighed. "Ah, I see. Well, the older we get, the more these things can affect the body. Healing takes longer, too. Which is why the laird needs to obey."

Duncan smirked. "Obey?"

Her cheeks heated. "Well, he needs to listen to me—and Malcolm—so he can have a full recovery."

"Ah."

Words kept tumbling out of her mouth, like she couldn't help herself. "If he listens, he won't have a limp when he walks again."

"I believe yer also callin' him, us…old?"

A twinkle in his eyes gave away the tease, but embarrassment made her face hotter.

It was Lila's turn to avert her gaze. "Not at all!" she blurted when she made herself look back at him.

Duncan wore a lopsided grin that made him look so much like Angus, her tummy wobbled.

She swallowed. Cleared her throat.

Neither helped.

"Uh…"

He chuckled and reached for her hand. "I jest, lass. I dinnae mean ta unsettle ye." His gaze was kind now, and Duncan studied her. "Are ye weel?"

Nod. Just nod.

Her internal order was barely followed. "Of course," she forced out. "Well, I'd better see to your brother. I need to check his stitches and the swelling." Lila fled up the stairs and around the corner without waiting for an answer.

chapter eight

Angus stormed back into the surgery right after Lila had run from him. "Ye!"

Startled hazel eyes met his gaze as Malcolm looked up from his mortar and pestle at one of his worktables. "Me?"

Angus frowned and closed the distance between them, ordering his hands to remain at his sides, instead of grabbing the man by his collar or punching him like he wanted. "Aye, *ye.*"

The older man straightened his shoulders and sat taller but didn't move off his stool. He lowered the tool in his hand. "Is there somethin' yer needin', Angus-lad?"

He'd always liked this man. However, repeating the idea wasn't helping at the moment. Angus wanted to command him to stay away from Lila. Or choke him. Or worse. "Ye've ne'er married," he blurted.

Confusion danced across the healer's face. "Wha' of it?" Malcolm cocked his head to one side, making his shaggy graying hair dance.

Angus paced in front of the long table. He was a complete idiot for bursting in here. For his jealousy. For letting his thoughts about his little healer get so twisted up, he was about to accuse a man he'd liked and respected his whole life of impropriety that likely didn't exist.

"Lad, is somethin' wrong?" Genuine concern wrapped the words, but it didn't calm him.

"Ye…are fond a' Lila, aye?" When he glanced at Malcolm, the older man's bushy brows were drawn tight. He took a breath, but it didn't help.

"Aye. As are ye. Are ye no'?"

Fond was too weak a word, but considering he barely knew her, it was more appropriate than the strong emotions swirling in his gut.

Angus didn't stop to call himself a fool…this time.

Lila was…his.

He wanted the healer to know that no matter how old the man was. "Aye," he barked.

Malcolm leaned back on the stool and appraised him. He crossed his arms over his chest, making his shirt seal itself to his rotund stomach. He'd filled out over the years.

After several moments of silence, the man smiled. Slowly. "I can guess wha' this…" the healer gestured between the two of them. "'Tis all about, lad."

Angus narrowed his eyes but chided himself for being rude. Tried not to fidget. "Nay, ye dinnae." He spoke the first words that came to mind, even if they sounded more like a whined denial than assertion, *he* was right, and Malcolm was wrong.

A chuckle drew his attention back to his apparent

rival's face, and Angus wanted to stab him. Or at least knock the smugness out of his smile.

"The lass…I'm fond a' her, aye, but tha same can be said of her. She's…fond a' me."

Angus startled, couldn't help it; hoped like hell the healer hadn't noticed.

Lila was fond of the older man?

Nay.

Perhaps that was why she'd pulled away from his kiss?

She kissed me back, first.

Angus wanted to shout it, although it was none of Malcolm's business that he'd kissed the physician from the future, and he sure as hell didn't want to admit to anyone aloud—or himself—that she'd shoved him away. Rejected him. Answered his confession to wanting her in the worst way possible, but declaring she didn't want him back. That he hadn't the *right* to kiss her.

However…she had kissed him back.

That means something, right?

"I ne'er married, 'tis true."

Malcolm's voice made Angus meet his eyes again.

He waited for the healer to continue.

"Mayhap 'twas, the right lass ne'er came along." His hazel gaze was sly, and he leaned back on his stool casually, as if he'd not just dropped a gauntlet at Angus' feet, even if just a verbal one.

Angus wanted to growl. Reach for his sword. Demand for Malcolm to explain what he'd just said, but he didn't want to hear the answer. Didn't dare ask what the healer's intentions were. If he did, depending on the answer, he just might blurt that Lila had kissed him. No need to share who'd initiated the intimacy.

If he girded his loins enough to ask, and the healer denied vying for Lila, Angus wouldn't likely believe him, and if he confessed, he wanted her, he'd want to kill him.

Had Malcolm put his hands on her?

He *would* kill him.

They'd been laughing together. They often spoke in close whispers, and when Lila was with Malcolm, she always wore a smile. Could she actually have some…*regard* for the healer, no matter his age and physical appearance?

The older man stared, and Angus fought the urge to pace the large room. His still-smug expression made his dark desires worse.

He'd have to win her.

He was younger, and although he'd never been a vain man, he was better looking than Malcolm had ever been, even in his prime.

If the healer thought he was competition for Lila's affections, Angus would have to prove him wrong.

He ignored Malcolm's chuckle when he hit the corridor, just like before, and slammed the surgery door with another growl.

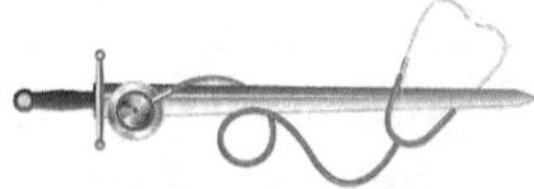

He answered the knock on his door with a holler to enter without looking up. Angus sat in a chair, staring into the dying fire in his hearth.

"I ran inta Lila in tha corridor taday." His uncle's words were even, but an obvious curiosity laced his voice that put Angus on edge as Duncan shut the thick panel and crossed the room.

"An'?" He tried to sound nonchalant.

"The lass looked…ravished."

Angus jerked on the end of the chair, then cursed his obvious reaction.

His uncle laughed.

He glared. Didn't dare say a word, but it didn't appear as if it mattered. "Malcolm tol' me perhaps he'd ne'er married 'cause tha right lass dinnae e'er come along."

Duncan arched an eyebrow when Angus couldn't suppress the hundredth growl for the day at the end of his statement.

"Is tha' right?"

Angus frowned. Nodded.

"Methinks tha man was tryin' ta make ye jealous, lad."

"Me? Jealous?" He startled again.

Duncan studied him. For so long, he squirmed in his seat.

"Sod off," Angus whispered.

Instead of being insulted, his uncle chuckled again. "So, why did tha lass look ravished?"

Angus didn't want to answer, so he looked away—again. "Sod off," he repeated, with his eyes on the hearth instead of his father's twin. The remaining small flames warmed his face—or so he told himself when embarrassment kissed the back of his neck.

More laughter greeted his ears, which made him scowl.

"Ye, lad, have go' it bad fer the little healer from tha future."

Again, a denial would get him nowhere—damn his meddling family—so Angus stuck to the silence that only made him stew more.

Duncan patting his shoulder made him jump and drew Angus' gaze back to the older man's face.

"'Tis weel an' good, ye ken."

"Meanin'?"

"The lass dinnae get here so long ago, I ken, but sometimes days is all it takes."

"Meanin'?" Angus repeated, but his pulse sped up.

His uncle smiled. "I ken Claire was mine tha moment my eyes landed on 'er."

Angus swallowed—couldn't help it. The statement was as bad as his mother's mantra about fate the night Lila had arrived.

Duncan wore a wistful smile that didn't look

right on a grizzled warrior's face. His graying five o'clock shadow matched his temples, and it was new growth, because his aunt didn't like facial hair. Most of the time his father's twin went clean-shaven.

"Naked on tha beach, like yer lass."

The memory of Lila's beautiful body bared made his heart jump.

He *wished* she was his lass but didn't want to voice that. Angus might've claimed her in his mind, but he didn't know how to make it true. He glanced back at the glowing embers instead of answering.

"Time dinnae matter. She's still my Claire-lass, an' has given me three braw laddies."

Angus expected Duncan to mention the dreaded phrase — *'love of his life'*, but he didn't.

"Considerin' the lass' locks were mussed an' her faced flushed pink, I'd say yer doin' jus' fine. Unless… 'ol Mal was tha culprit."

Angus whipped around and glared.

His uncle laughed so hard, his eyes watered, and he slapped his thigh. Duncan shook his head, making his long hair dance. "I s'pose 'twas ye after all. Good lad."

He didn't want to sulk again, but for the fourth — or was it the fiftieth — time he chose not to answer, and looked at the fire again. Studied every piece of ash, and wished the power to make someone disappear was a part of his magic.

Angus could command him to leave, but his

uncle would likely laugh harder while ignoring him. He wanted to roll his eyes—something his sister did daily.

"Somethin' wrong, lad?" Real concern threaded Duncan's words, but he still didn't spare him a glance.

"Sod off," Angus whispered again, but a heavy hand landed on his shoulder and squeezed.

"I was jus' teasin ye, Angus-lad. I dinnae intend ta upset ye."

"Ye dinnae," he denied.

His uncle flashed a knowing smile but didn't contradict him—thank Jesus. "Dinnae fash o'er what Malcolm Beaton tol' ye. The man could ne'er hold a candle ta ye. If tha lass wants a man, 'tis ye."

Angus snorted.

Should he thank him?

"I'll bid ye g'night, lad."

He nodded by way of answer, and soon Duncan retreated without another word. He remained where he was long after his uncle had shut the door.

Angus should bar it to avoid other visitors, even if the hour grew late and anyone else was unlikely.

He wanted Lila to come to his room.

She'd denied wanting him, so it wouldn't have a purpose, would it?

He closed his eyes and stifled a yawn.

Why was he taking her rejection so hard?

Angus was sitting in his room, sulking like a laddie denied a bannock or sweet cake.

A sigh breeched his lips when his mother's voice tickled his mind—words from the night his little healer had arrived in his century.

"Perhaps the lass is your fate, as your father is mine."

Well, if Lila was, they certainly weren't off to a good start.

chapter nine

►► "Where do you think you're going, my laird?" Lila added the honorific belatedly to soften the demand. After all, she shouldn't rudely order the man around; he was the respected leader of his clan. Even still, she was his doctor, and right now, *she* was the boss.

Too bad Alex MacLeod hadn't gotten the memo.

The older man froze on the edge of his bed and pinned her with a wide-eyed, *oh shit* — or shite, as he'd say — sapphire stare. He averted his gaze, and his cheeks were tinged pink.

She blinked.

Lila had made him *blush?*

Well, at least he knew he shouldn't be getting up or trying to walk. It was way too soon.

The laird didn't answer, just eased back into his bed, wearing a grimace.

Whether it was embarrassment or discomfort, Lila didn't guess at, but she wasn't above teasing him. "Does that hurt? *Good.* You're not ready. It's only been a week."

A disgruntled frown downturned his mouth but Alex didn't glare, as she'd expected.

He still didn't speak, as if he didn't know what to

say. Caught like a teenager trying to sneak out of the house.

Lila felt, rather than heard, Angus' approach. Awareness prickled down her spine, and she cursed it. Refused to turn toward him.

"Da." His voice was exasperated, and her peripheral vision picked up her rescuer running his hand through his long dark locks. "Ye've *go'* ta listen ta Lila."

Another shiver hit when he said her name. It rolled off his tongue like a caress.

Every. Damn. Time.

She hated herself for reacting. No good could come from this…fascination…with Angus MacLeod. No matter how many times Lila had told herself to ignore the draw, she failed to do so as soon as he walked into a room.

It'd only gotten worse since he'd kissed her. Days ago—which felt like hours or minutes with all the obsessing she'd done about it.

Weak fool.

Lila swallowed a growl. She hated appearing weak, even in her own mind.

"Dinnae think ta tell me wha' ta do." The laird frowned up at his son, but there was no bite in his words.

Guilt, maybe?

"I *am* gonna have *Màthair* keep ye asleep wi' magic." Angus waggled his finger, and his father batted his hand away.

"Do you wish to have a permanent limp, my laird?" Lila said in her sensible, *I'm-right-you're-wrong* tone.

Alex aimed his frown in her direction. His eyes said, *nay*, even though he still didn't address her.

She bit back a smirk, lest she piss him off.

"Yer lass is o'erbearin', lad." He was looking at her but spoke to his son.

Lila stilled; couldn't glance at Angus. She needed to assert she was *not* his lass, or his *anything*, but the words wouldn't come.

"She dinnae be *wrong*, Da."

The man she was avoiding gazing upon saved her, but she should've had issue with *him* not correcting his father, too.

Right?

Lila cleared her throat. "I can have Malcolm tell you, if you'd prefer." She arched an eyebrow in a dare and hollered at herself to get it together. Couldn't—or *shouldn't*—let a little comment throw her off like that.

Besides, the laird hadn't meant anything by the possessive, had he?

The man couldn't actually believe she and Angus were...involved?

He only kissed me, and I told him no.

It wasn't like she could voice any of that, even if she wanted to. Which Lila most certainly did *not*.

"Dinnae be necessary," Alex muttered.

"I'll go get *Màthair*," Angus said, gesturing toward the door with his thumb. His expression was innocent enough, but mischief danced in his eyes.

"Nay." The laird's word was too fast, as if his son had threatened him, and Lila bit back a smile.

"Then I can get on with my exam?" she asked, feigning an innocence that matched her rescuer's.

"Aye," Alex said, but his blue gaze was narrowed in her direction.

Again, she fought her amusement. He really was like a little kid, just like his wife had worried about when Lila had done his surgery a week before.

She hoped he hadn't tried to put any weight on his leg when she wasn't there to catch him. "How many times have you tried to get out of bed?" she asked instead, trying to keep her voice light, instead of accusatory.

"Och, ye sound like my wife," Alex complained.

"She's right. *I'm* right. I know it sucks, but you need to ob—listen, my laird." Lila nixed the word *obey*. Big strong guys like Alex didn't take well to it.

A voice whispered that neither did his son, but she tried to ignore it, as well as the magnetic draw to the man by her side. It was a constant battle, worse since his mouth had been on hers.

She shivered. Lila had been obsessing about their kiss, no matter how she yelled at herself. She'd started dreaming of Angus that same night—doing a hell of a lot more than kissing.

It couldn't happen.

Wouldn't.

She was going home as soon as his father was back on his feet. Alana had promised such, and Lila had her fellowship, her friends, and the hospital to return to.

Lila had tried not to worry about all the surgeries she'd missed on the schedule in the seven days she'd been in 1692. Nothing that'd been an emergency, but surely Lizzie and Sophie had freaked out when she'd gone.

Lila had disappeared.

They'd called the police, right?

Reported her missing.

The tour group leader had cautioned them to stay together and had told them when to meet back at the bus so they could tour Dunvegan.

Well, she'd *stayed* with her friends. The Faery Stones had interfered and sucked her back in time. Lila believed Alana; the former princess and the rest of the MacLeods would get her back to where she belonged, but she couldn't leave yet.

She had a patient here, and Alex needed her.

Despite his grousing.

Angus' shoulder brushed hers, and she jolted.

Lila didn't spare him a peep—she couldn't. She leaned down and put her hand on the laird's leg, carefully prodding his sutures.

Alex's brow drew tight, but he didn't comment or

express pain.

"These look good. Perhaps another week, give or take a few days, and they can come out."

"Good," the laird said.

"The swelling looks much better, too. If you stay *off* of it, like you're *supposed* to, that should continue, and we should have a better picture of when you can walk." Lila tightened the ties on the wooden slats that made up his splint, and Angus' father hissed.

A curse slid from his lips, and he muttered an apology, since she was a lady.

She flashed a smile. "No worries." When he looked at her, she schooled her expression. She wanted him to know she was serious. "Broken bones generally take about eight weeks to heal, remember that. Yours is worse since the fracture was compound—the bone broke through your skin and tore muscle on the way out. You can't push it, or you could injure yourself worse. Worse than a limp."

Alex offered a nod, but it had a reluctant edge.

Lila's gut said it wasn't because he didn't believe her; he just didn't like what she said.

Angus' eyes burned from beside her.

Their gazes brushed, and his expression made her flush. He peered down at her with something akin to respect—or wonder.

She tingled all over, but she swallowed, forcing her focus back on her patient. "How's your pain?"

"I'm hale." Alex's mouth was a hard line, with

only the slightest tremor.

"Don't be an action hero. If it hurts, speak up. Malcolm has meds that can help."

The two men exchanged a look that told Lila they hadn't a clue what she'd just said.

"Sorry, I just mean, don't push yourself, my laird. There's no reason to deal with the pain when we have a remedy at hand. Rest, will help."

Angus muttered something about sleep being the only guarantee his father would behave, and Alex glared.

Lila hid a smile. "If only we could put you out like Sleeping Beauty, and you'd wake up healed."

They exchanged another look, and she sighed.

"It's a story about…oh, never mind." She shook her head.

Alex smirked. "There's been many a time o'er tha years when Claire's said somethin' tha' dinnae make sense."

"I get it. I guess it's hard to remember *when* I am." Lila offered a small smile. Surprise washed over her when the truth of her words hit home.

She'd been in the seventeenth century for a week, yet she'd found some normality in her situation. Lila had a patient, and even if she didn't have morning rounds like at the hospital, she'd quickly fallen into a routine here.

Malcolm's surgery and checking in with the healer was the first stop after eating each morning—

and she'd actually made more time for regular meals here. Then she always visited Alex for a morning exam and chat.

Hospital days had eaten up her existence for so long in the "real" world, and she usually got nagged by coworkers and friends for skipping meals. Lila was a doctor after all, who knew better, especially with how busy she was. She commonly subsisted on coffee. Perhaps there were advantages to being in the past.

After her daily hour or so with the laird, sometimes she spent time with the females at Dunvegan, and sometimes she returned to her new colleague and helped him with whatever he had on his agenda.

She'd assisted him with supplies, made poultices, took notes, prepared draughts, and done another dozen things that would've made her grandmother beam.

Lila had helped him treat his regular patients, too. Some came to see Malcolm for chronic conditions, and of course there were other emergencies like Alex's, but nothing as serious. She'd sutured a knife wound for a kitchen maid the other day, and of course there were minor injuries from the men on the fighting yard, but most didn't want to be doctored for wounds gained when training.

She liked watching Malcolm in action. His natural solutions for things like arthritis, migraines and indigestion were a wonder to hear. His manner was gentle and direct, and he knew more about holistic meds — of course, his only choice — than her *lita*.

He was a man to admire, respect — and she did, very much. He had a quick wit and a calming quality that always made her feel better instantly. He made her laugh, and she enjoyed spending time with him, healing with him. Malcolm wasn't hot tempered like her, so they made a good team.

The only blip in her new structure was standing beside her.

Lila could feel Angus' eyes on her again and she tried to banish her constant cognizance — and reaction — to those sapphire orbs pointing in her direction. She fought a shiver for good measure.

Lila didn't always see him first thing in the morning like this one, but he was always on her mind.

Unfortunately.

Since he'd been haunting her dreams, she'd discovered she *wanted* to see him, in the mornings or otherwise.

They hadn't discussed their kiss, and Angus hadn't tried to kiss her again, but she craved sharing words with him, if only polite conversation. Avoidance regarding what'd happened between them was of course the way to go, and it couldn't happen again, so it shouldn't matter, right? So why was it bothering her?

You're a glutton for punishment.

Lila had told him she didn't want him; maybe that was why he'd maintained a respectful distance?

She wanted him to kiss her again. She wanted to explore her dreams.

Those truths weren't budging, no matter the amount of self-deprecation she lumped on.

"I hope tha' means ye can an' have found some happiness here."

Alex's voice made her jump.

Lila was so lost in her own thoughts; she didn't hear him at first. Like he was far away. She cleared her throat. "I have, thanks," she answered the laird, but looked at his son. Couldn't help it.

chapter ten

ila sighed and scooted the chair back from the desk. "I give up. This is hard as hell." She glanced at her hands. Dark, angry blotches spattered her index fingers—both of them. Not to mention her thumbs, and the skin between. She flipped her palms up. Stains were there, too. Only this time, not blood.

Her gaze darted over all the crumpled clumps of parchment surrounding the small desk in the ledger room.

The laird had told her she was welcome to use his office to write a letter for Sophie and Lizzie.

Lila had been in the 17th century for two weeks and wouldn't be able to leave Alex's care for weeks to come. When she'd worried about her friends, Xander had suggested she write a note, sans the time travel of course, and he'd make sure it got to where it needed to go. The former Fae Warrior had vowed he wouldn't let her down.

He'd explained he'd need Liam's help, since his son was half-human, but the boy had hurriedly agreed to assist in any way he could. Probably out of guilt.

It didn't have to be complicated. Just something to let her friends know she was okay. Only wanted to write it on one line actually—

I'm safe. I'll be back soon. –L.

Hell if Lila could manage writing even that with a quill and dipping it in ink. She had too much, or not enough. Huge illegible blotches or barely readable strokes. She'd wasted tons of parchment. Something she had a feeling was rather precious around here. What she wouldn't give for a freaking pen.

"Somethin' wrong, lass?"

The deep voice, laced with amusement shot awareness down her spine.

Dammit.

The last thing Lila needed was for him to *know* he'd startled her.

How long had Angus been watching her?

"Of course not."

Disbelief colored those sapphire eyes. He leaned on the doorframe as if he hadn't a care in the world, huge arms crossed over his massive chest—all his muscles bulging. "Are ye sure?"

Lila frowned.

He smirked.

She wasn't about to ask Angus MacLeod for *help*. Especially not when he was looking at her like that. Besides, to get help with writing would mean he had to get close. *Close* didn't work for her avoidance plan.

It'd been working so far—sorta. Lila still saw him every day. If not more than once, at least at evening meal when all the men were done on the fighting yard.

Unfortunately, the end of the day was when he was most tempting. Usually freshly bathed, with clean clothing and damp hair, her fingers itched to smooth. Not to mention, Angus smelled so damn good. She wanted his scent—and his hands—all over her. No matter how Lila denied it.

"Did you need something?" The intended bark came out more like a whisper that made her cringe. There was no way he wouldn't be able to tell how much he unsettled her.

Angus just stared, and the longer he neglected to speak, the faster her heart beat.

Her eyes landed on his mouth. Against her will, his taste drifted into her mind.

He cleared his throat and she jumped.

Then cursed herself.

"Did ye get any ink on tha parchment?"

"What?"

With two strides, he closed the distance to her. They seemed to glance at her stained fingertips at the same time.

When Angus reached for her, Lila yanked away and shoved her hands under her ass.

He chuckled and shook his head, his lopsided grin making her insides wobble, even though she tried to banish the sensation.

The current piece of parchment on the desk had one letter on it. A messy, too-much-ink, *I*.

Lila avoided looking there, since he'd already noticed it, and ignored her hands going numb from her weight. "I'm a surgeon. I'm usually good with my hands."

His eyes shot back to hers so fast it made her head spin.

She gulped—actually frickin' gulped.

Way to insert-foot-in-mouth, Lila.

Then again, *'insert'* was a bad word, too. Lila fidgeted on the chair until the legs rocked her back a few feet.

Away from him.

Which was what she needed.

Her neck scorched, until the heat spread to her face, all the way up to her ears.

Angus cleared his throat again. "Ah, weel, it takes practice. Give me yer hand."

"Wh—no. I—can do it."

Please, God, tell me I didn't stutter that out, did I?

A thick arched eyebrow disagreed. "Yer wastin' good parchment."

Guilt cast her eyes to her lap, and Lila released her hands from their prison. "I'm sorry, you're right. I should've asked for help."

"I can write it fer ya."

"No, they know my handwriting. It has to be me."

Angus nodded and picked up the quill.

Leaned too close for her comfort to grab it. Lila

had the squirms again.

His essence tickled her nose, and even tinged with sweat he appealed.

She fought the urge to curse herself again and sucked in another breath. What she'd meant to calm her racing pulse only filled her olfactory system with more of *him* and had the opposite effect. She couldn't get the memory of his mouth on hers to go away.

"Ye have ta knock the ink off, like this."

Lila jarred but hollered at herself to listen.

With patience and efficient strokes, Angus showed her, then helped her form the letters of her two short sentences, first with his big hand around hers before Lila did it on her own.

She was so distracted she had no clue how she'd managed it, but soon, *'I'm safe. I'll be back soon. –L.'* stared up from the rough paper, and the penmanship was passable as hers. She beamed up at him. "Thank you so much. This probably would've taken me until supper."

Angus laughed, a warm sound that encased her, and scattered her thoughts all over again.

They stared at each other, and her breath stalled when he dipped toward her ever so slightly, as if waiting for an invitation.

"Any time, lass." His voice was thick, full of obvious desire.

Panic lanced through her and made the heat of his proximity, his words, his smile, his *everything,* evaporate. Lila shot to her feet, abandoned her letter, and fled the ledger room.

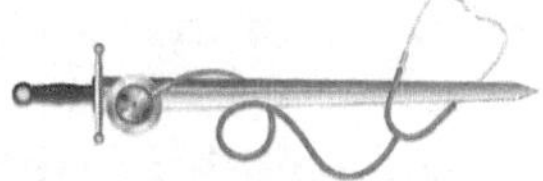

"Lila! Malcolm! Help! Come quick!"

The surgery door flew open, and Lila looked up when she heard the panic in Lexi's voice.

The girl's violet eyes were so wide the whites peeked, and she was shaking from head to toe.

Malcolm reached her first and seized her by the shoulders. "Calm, lassie."

She fought his hold and grabbed his shirt with one desperate hand. "Ye have ta come! My Da!"

Lila rushed past them and out of the room. She didn't need to hear more.

I am not going to lose another patient.

She took the stairs two at a time and pushed past the burn in her lungs to go faster, around the corner and up the last stairwell, dashing down the wide hallway to the laird's quarters. Didn't stop, no matter the surprised MacLeods she passed.

The laird's daughter must've left the door open when she'd fled the room, because Lila darted inside without needing to slow.

Alex was sitting on the floor, against his bed, moaning and pale, cradling his injured leg to his chest, splints, and all.

That wasn't the most concerning part.

There was a small pool of blood at his feet.

"Alex!" Lila sucked in air when she screeched to a halt before him. She didn't have time to double over and pant with her hands on her knees like her body begged for.

"Da!" Angus appeared in the doorway, his mother on his heels.

"Quick, help me get him back in bed." The cursory glance told her the sutures were decimated. She wouldn't know if he'd damaged the bone and muscle repair job until she got him prone for another look.

Without a word, Angus supported his father's weight and helped her haul him back onto the large bed. His grimace was grave, and Lila wanted to reassure him, but made herself concentrate on the laird.

"What did you do?" Alana demanded.

"Not now, let me have a look at him." Lila's heart thundered and she forced herself to breathe. Besides his pallor, Alex's life wasn't in danger, so she could release her emergent senses, but her mental gears were in overdrive.

His bleeding could be controlled, like before. They had yarrow, among other things. Malcolm had poultices prepped, there would be no waiting.

The healer came into the room with his doctor's satchel on his shoulder. He was out of breath, and his torso heaved. His hair was mussed, and his spectacles hung partially off his face. He righted them and joined her beside Alex.

Lexi entered as well, and went to her mother, sniffling quietly.

Her brother snagged her arm and pulled her into him, wrapping her in a tight embrace. "'Twill be all right, lass," Angus whispered.

Lila blocked them all out and looked at her colleague.

The older man handed her sanitized thread without a word and dug through his bag again. He produced a clean white cloth for her.

"What happened, my laird?" she asked, trying to keep her voice light. Her pulse had finally evened from her run, and the knee-jerk concern. She wiped the blood away from the tear in Alex's leg so she could assess the damage.

The man hissed.

Lila tried not to glare as their eyes met. "You've made a mess of this, so I hope it was worth it."

Alex grimaced and shook his head. "I dinnae be a bairn." He crossed his arms over his chest.

Alana approached the bedside. Most of the time when she did so, she reached for her husband's hand, but this time she perched them on her hips and her violet eyes shot daggers at him. "Then stop actin' like one. Lila and Malcolm do not tell you things for the pleasure of it. What do you have to say for yourself?"

He averted his gaze from her irritation, and Lila had to hide a smile.

She surveyed his wound. Only one of the twenty or so sutures was still in place, but the bleeding had slowed on its own. She was going to have to look inside to make sure he hadn't splintered his bone again. "Did you put any weight on your leg? Don't lie to me."

"Aye." His voice was low, the word wrapped in discomfort.

"Did you try to walk?"

"Nay, dinnae hold me. I fell." Alex scowled. The man's frustration permeated the room.

Lila believed him, considering how close he'd been to his bed. "Patience, my laird. Healing takes time, no matter how much in a hurry we are. We can't rush it, try as we might; it's only been two weeks. You'll be back on your feet soon. If you *listen*. I have to check something before I can sew you up again, and it's going to hurt." So much for taking his stitches out in the next day or two, which had been her plan. The laird had just started the whole healing process over, whether he knew it or not.

Alex frowned, then looked at his wife.

"Do not look at me for magical help, my laird. You did this to yourself. *You* must bear the consequences." She crossed her arms over her breasts. Her beautiful face was tight with ire.

Alana was *pissed*.

All the time Lila had been there, the woman had only referred to her husband with his title when she was angry. She hid another smile, and Malcolm cleared his throat, poorly disguising a laugh.

Angus smirked when Lila looked up and caught his eye, but his sister still wore an expression of distress as she rested her dark head on his chest.

Jealousy swirled in her gut and she hollered at herself. They were siblings for Godssakes, and he only comforted her.

Lila needed to concentrate on what she was doing anyway and forget about the forbidden…the memory of Angus' kiss. How that chest felt against her breasts when he'd pressed her into the wall. How big and warm his hands felt on her back and waist, on her ass, even through clothing.

Knock it off. Get to work.

She had a patient, and her fingers were covered in blood. Now was *not* the time to fantasize about a man she wouldn't let herself have. "Well, say a prayer, my laird," Lila said when she was finished checking him internally. "Your fall only ripped your stitches. The bone and muscle are still where they're supposed to be. They look good, in fact. The bleeding has mostly stopped, but you've added some recovery time. I was hoping to get you up on crutches, but we'll have to wait now."

"How much longer?" Alex gritted out.

She pointed to his leg, then the mattress. "I'd say you purchased yourself another two weeks, if not three, right here in this bed."

He cursed.

Alana harrumphed.

The laird made a noise in his throat, but very pointedly avoided his wife's gaze.

Lila shrugged and wiped her hands on a clean cloth Malcolm handed her.

The healer gave her the needle and she threaded it quickly, shooting her patient another look. "Brace yourself, this won't be comfortable. And I need you to be still."

Alex's curses continued with every stroke, but she got the job done with minimal movement from him.

She cleaned off his leg and stepped aside for Malcolm to apply a new poultice. Because of the pressure he'd put on the break, the swelling had returned.

The older man instructed his laird as he worked—soft-spoken and gentle as always. The opposite of Lila's approach, given that Alex had done something stupid.

Claire and Janet joined them—likely due to the commotion, and Janet cleaned up her brother's blood.

One of Claire and Duncan's boys, Rory, hovered in the doorway. Their middle child resembled Claire the most, despite Iain being the only fair-haired one. He had her green eyes, too, which were striking with his dark hair.

Lila thought he was sixteen or seventeen, and

there was no doubt girls would chase him from all over, if they weren't already.

"I dinnae need tha whole clan in here," Alex groused, gesturing in a circle. He crossed his arms, again.

Angus snorted.

Lexi went to her father's side and held his hand.

His expression softened when he looked at his daughter, and she leaned down to kiss his cheek and whisper something in Gaelic.

Alana made a noise and arched a delicate fair eyebrow. Clearly, she'd not forgiven her husband for his foolish attempt to walk without assistance on a two-week-old broken bone.

"Complainin' will get ye nowhere," Janet said as she straightened and put the bloody rags in a basket in the corner. "Perhaps next time, cleanin' up after yerself will change yer tune." She cocked her head to one side and narrowed her eyes.

Lila pursed her lips to keep a laugh in. At least his whole family was on *her* side; she didn't really need to fuss at Alex. The MacLeod women were brilliant enough, as Sophie would say.

Claire shook her head but wore a smile. "Alex, I didn't realize you're as stubborn as Duncan. I thought you were the more reasonable twin."

Alana made an unladylike noise in her throat.

The laird scowled.

Lila couldn't help but smile, too. She felt someone

looking at her, and her gaze collided with Angus'.

He was looking — no, *staring* — in her direction.

Her heart skipped. Another breath didn't keep her libido from zinging awake. She'd been cataloging fresh herbs for Malcolm down in the surgery before the laird's scare, and she'd been super interested in the task, but now she didn't want to return to boring herbalism.

Lila wanted to spend the rest of the afternoon with Angus.

She admonished herself and helped gather the rest of the supplies, dumping them in the healer's bag. She left the room first, slinging the satchel over her shoulder and telling Malcolm she'd see him in his domain.

Lila reminded Alana to come get her if they needed anything.

It wasn't often she fled a patient's side, but she needed to get away from Angus.

She *almost* made it down to the surgery. She was on the last set of stairs, when footsteps behind her made her pause. That same awareness from upstairs shot down her spine.

Lila wanted to run to him and push him away at the same time.

What's wrong with me?

"Lila." Her name was soft yet immobilizing.

She glanced over her shoulder and watched Angus come to her.

They were utterly *alone*.

His size ate up all the air in the hallway, and the walls seemed to pulse, like they were going to close in.

Lila fought shudders. Not because she was afraid, but because every inch of her body thrummed for the big Highlander.

"Lila," Angus repeated. He extended his arms, as if he would reach for her, but then lowered them to his sides.

Disappointment made her bite her bottom lip.

"Thank ye, again, fer fixin' my stubborn git of a da." His eyes were so serious. So blue, so beautiful. Then he smiled.

A tiny thing, and her whole form responded again; her case of the tingles, the wants, worsened.

"I won't say it was my pleasure, because if he'd listen to me, there wouldn't have been an issue, but you're welcome."

Silence fell, but Angus offered her a nod.

"Lila—"

"Angus—"

They spoke at the same time.

Then they laughed.

Somehow the tension snapped, but Lila was still on edge—with yearning. "Go ahead," she whispered.

"Nay, ye, lass."

She shook her head. Didn't know what she wanted to say, anyway. It wasn't like she could tell him, *"Hey, I know I pushed you away, but I want to jump your bones."* She shivered at the pictures — her dreams — the idea planted in her head.

He tilted his chin up, as if he could read her mind. Angus took an audible breath and pinned her with an intense gaze.

Lila was vaguely aware that they were only a foot from where he'd kissed her the first time.

"Why're ye always runnin' from me, lass?" He kept his voice low, steady.

The question made her heart stutter, then thunder. She had no words, so she only stared.

Angus licked his bottom lip, obviously waiting for her to come up with *something.*

Watching his mouth only made her sear. Lila averted her gaze as her own throat went dry, her tongue glued to the roof of her mouth. Her eyes skimmed the contents of the bag on her arm. She'd not closed the flap when she'd grabbed it up and escaped the laird's suite.

"I wanna ken what yer thinkin'."

"I—" Lila's voice cracked. When clearing her throat didn't make the words come, she whirled away and did what Angus had just accused — she ran for Malcolm's surgery.

chapter eleven

a sigh fell from his lips as Angus watched her go. He wouldn't go after her; it would do no good. Hell, she'd probably barred the door to the surgery. He shook his head and turned to ascend the stairs.

His little healer had run from him again.

She'd avoided his gaze the whole time he'd been in his father's suite — granted she'd been busy with the laird. Still, she wouldn't look at Angus, even after things had calmed.

Kissing her hadn't gotten him anywhere. Now, Lila shied away from him, even if they touched by accident. Especially then.

His hand had touched hers when passing bread at midday meal, and she'd yanked back as if he'd flayed her open.

She went out of her way *not* to touch him when *he'd* wanted nothing more.

Then the dreams…

Angus dreamed of her nightly. Vivid and erotic visions, leaving him hard and aching when he woke, and his hand couldn't do an adequate job of relieving the drive, the need of her.

Only being with Lila like he'd fantasized would quench his desire. Maybe if he could have her, the dreams would stop.

Was there a purpose to them beyond torturing him?

His mother's words haunted him.

Fate.

Fate?

Considering the circumstances, how could that be true, when his little healer couldn't seem to stand being near Angus?

Lila had retreated from his father's rooms, leaving the poor man to female MacLeod fussing, and without really even saying goodbye to anyone—except Malcolm.

Angus frowned.

They'd never discussed the kiss. Any time he'd thought he might be able to bring it up, she'd move away as if he was a leper. He couldn't have such a conversation publicly, so he'd given up, ignoring the hurt throbbing in the back of his mind.

Each time Lila avoided him made her denial of wanting him scorch a little more, from the inside out. No amount of commanding himself to let it go was helping. No amount of calling himself a fool had an effect, either.

His memories of her taste and his dreams seconded that.

Angus sighed again and crossed the great hall.

He should return to the fighting yard. His cousin Lachlan had challenged him to a sparring duel, and he needed to teach the lad a lesson.

Lan, as most called him, was newly twenty, and sometimes carried an ego too big for his breeches. He was decent with a sword, aye, but Angus was better. As was their cousin Liam, so the lads often had to best each other for bragging rights, and perhaps a wager or two.

"Lad, may I have a word?" Uncle Duncan called. He stood near the largest hearth, with obvious worry wrinkled on his forehead.

He went to his father's twin without delay. "Somethin' wrong, Uncle?"

"Truth be tol', I'm concerned o'er yer da."

"Stubborn git," they said at the same time, then exchanged wry smiles.

"Lila will have Da on tha mend in no time."

Duncan tilted is head, as if he needed to think on it, then offered a curt nod. "I can only hope so. There's somethin' I need ye ta do fer me."

"Anathin'."

"I'm due ta retrieve an order tha lasses made months ago, fabrics tha' come from France. 'Tis a big supply, ta get us new clothin' fer the year or more; gowns fer the lasses, a' course. Tha steward an' tha cook also ordered some items we dinnae see oft'. 'Tis in Inverness."

"Inverness?" They only made the trip a few times

a year, The three or four-day ride would likely be longer with a cart. Angus would need one, with a bevy that large.

"Aye, I'd lead tha party, but since yer da dinnae be weel, my place needs ta be here."

Angus nodded; he understood and appreciated his uncle stepping in to handle his father's duties, so he wouldn't have to.

It wasn't that he didn't want to help his clan, or that he didn't know the laird's responsibilities—he'd been training under his father's tutelage for years. He'd be laird when the time came, and without complaint. However, at the moment he'd rather chase Lila.

Lila.

His little healer didn't *want* to be chased—which made Angus want her more.

Maybe if he left for a while, his feelings would fade?

"I'll go."

Duncan smiled; relief stamped all over his expression. "I ken ye would. Thank ye."

"'Tis my duty."

His uncle offered another curt nod. "Cormac'll go wit' ye, a' course, an' ye can take as many men as ye want. My lads may want ta go, except Iain, Claire dinnae be havin' that."

The older blond man was their cousin and had been in charge of all the MacLeod men-at-arms under

Duncan's purview as war chief for years. He was younger than his father and uncle — although, not by much — and one of the best trackers of the clan. Angus had always been fond of him and had learned many a skill from him since childhood.

"Aye, sounds good. When do we need ta leave?"

"Nay later than tha morn."

"I understand. Make sure Da dinnae act a fool while I'm gone."

Duncan flashed a grin. "I suspicion tha' duty is better left ta yer mother an' our little physician from tha future."

Angus ignored how his gut wobbled at the mention of Lila. Forced a laugh. "Aye, perhaps."

His uncle arched an eyebrow. "Somethin' wrong?"

"Nay," he said quickly. Too fast, if the man's expression was any indication. Words tumbled out of his mouth. "Do ye think there's a jeweler in Inverness?"

"Aye, I know a' one. Why?"

"No reason. I'm gonna need his name."

Duncan answered, but studied Angus until he practically fled his side.

Perhaps he was picking up a lesson from Lila.

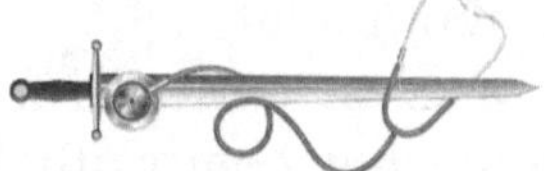

When Lila reached the great hall, the MacLeods sat around the great table, already eating breakfast.

Claire offered a smile as she passed her youngest son the basket of bannocks, and Duncan winked at Lila.

The laird's chair next to Alana was still empty, but it shouldn't be more than a few weeks until Alex was able to join them, provided Lila could get him some crutches and train him to really keep the weight off the break.

Also provided he didn't pull another stunt like he had the previous day and add more healing time or the need for another re-suturing. With as much pain as he'd suffered, Lila assumed her patient had learned his lesson.

Let us all hope.

She couldn't remember if they'd have crutches in 1692. They'd probably covered the origin of the simple device in med school, but courses and classrooms felt like ages ago, so her mind was blank on the subject.

Considering the current century, med school as Lila knew it was a long time away anyway. Just in the future instead of the past. She shut down time-continuum thoughts. Trying to figure it all out made her temples ache.

A cane wouldn't work for Alex, so they might have to come up with a crutches design anyway, but she'd have to see about it later.

The former princess gestured for Lila to have a seat, but there were a few chairs other than the laird's left empty.

She was only concerned with one in particular.

"Where's Angus?" she blurted.

"He went down to Inverness to handle some clan business," Claire said. "My lads are with him."

Several sets of eyes landed on Lila after she'd found her normal spot, and she wanted to fidget. Did they know something she didn't?

Why did you ask about him?

Now that his aunt had answered, Lila had a dozen questions she wanted to ask. Things that were none of her business.

It didn't matter that her Highlander — *no, stop.*

Angus *wasn't* hers, and she needed to erase that notion from her brain.

It didn't matter that *the* handsome Highlander had gone away.

Inverness was only a few hours' bus-ride in her century, but 1692 travel standards meant he'd be gone a while.

Her heart sped up and she stared down at the full trencher Janet handed her, mumbling thanks when Liam, Janet's son, passed her the warm bannocks and honey butter.

Why did Lila care?

Angus wasn't her concern. She was only there to care for his father, and she was doing so.

Somehow, the routine she'd been grateful for in the two weeks she'd been in 1692 didn't matter. Even if it wasn't first thing in the morning, she always saw the laird's son. Daily.

Looked forward to it. She…needed his smile. His blue eyes. His deep voice.

Stop it, Lila.

Angus hadn't tried to kiss her again, even though she always saw—maybe *felt*—him watching her. Especially from her peripheral vision when she didn't have the guts to face him. She seemed to always know where he was, and vice versa.

The day before, she'd run from him—as he'd adequately accused her of. Since he'd kissed her, and she couldn't get a handle on his magnetism, Lila *had* been running from him.

Angus was too tempting.

The joke was on her, though. Every night since then, she'd dreamt of him, and all the naughty things they *shouldn't*—couldn't—*wouldn't, dammit*—do together.

She was infatuated.

Completely clouded by lust.

He'd seen her naked on the beach, and she couldn't say the same of Angus unclothed, but her imagination was freaking fantastic. Better than any subscription television service. Totally ridiculous.

Lila shuddered and forced a bite of bread into her mouth. The bannock was thick and the flavor of honey wrapped around her tongue, but it wasn't as sweet as Angus' mouth on hers.

Seriously, Lila, knock it off.

She wanted to roll her eyes at herself.

"Are you well, lass?"

The smooth voice belonged to Alana, and she wanted to fidget even more.

"A-a-ye."

Stuttering?

Perfect.

Now Xander's gaze—among others at the table—was on her, too. He could read minds, and she *so* didn't need that right now.

Lila's neck heated, so she reached for a goblet of mead and sipped while avoiding everyone's collective stares.

"Have ye seen tha laird yet this morn?" Janet asked.

She zoned in on Angus' aunt's blue eyes and wanted to shout her thanks. She could kiss the woman for helping her focus on what she *should* be thinking about anyway.

Much better than Angus.

Lila promptly ignored the little voice in the back of her head that called her a liar. A big, fat one, too. "I went up, but he was still sleeping, so I'll go back with Malcolm when I'm done with breakfast. I didn't want to disturb him, but I do need to check the new sutures. I'm worried about infection, since he reopened the wound."

"I put him to sleep with a spell," Alana said matter-of-factly as she sipped water.

Duncan snorted.

Lila caught a few headshakes in her peripheral vision.

"You cannot just leave him asleep, Alana," Xander barked.

"I can, and I will, until he stops acting like a fool."

The laird's twin chuckled. "Then I s'pose my brother shall sleep fer eternity."

There were a few laughs around the table, and Lila sighed.

Obviously, *Her Highness* was not over Alex's attempt to walk yesterday.

"While I can see the merit, can't he come to harm from such…a spell?" Lila asked. It was still hard to swallow that magic was real, and they were discussing it openly, at the breakfast table in the great hall.

Claire had told her the close clan members were long aware of it, and comfortable. She'd also said Alana had magic in place to prevent the frivolous mention of it to the wrong ears, and that was mostly meant for servants who didn't live within Dunvegan's confines.

Angus had said there were rumors all over the place anyway. Said there wouldn't be fairy tales, otherwise.

"Not likely," Xander answered. "But that does *not* make it right."

"I shall care for my husband as I see fit," Alana

said in a regal tone that brooked no argument.

The fair-haired Fae man pursed his lips and shook his head.

Alana was Alex's wife, but Lila was his doctor. Magic was out of her element, so she didn't know if she should be alarmed or push the issue. "How long has he been asleep?" she ventured.

"Since last eve."

"Alana." Her name was all warning, and Xander narrowed his eyes. "Wake him. Do not wait until you're done breaking your fast. Go upstairs and do it. Now."

Silence at the table was thick, and the rising tension palpable as the MacLeods exchanged looks. Evidently, only her cousin would dare order the former princess around.

"Nay." Alana didn't look at the man as she answered. Her violet stare landed on Lila. "If you have need to converse with my husband, I shall wake him. Not before then. In his current state, he cannot harm himself."

Lila couldn't argue with that. *Sorta.* "Well, he does need to stay hydrated. And protein will help him heal."

The laird's wife nodded. "It shall be done. Later."

Lila bit her bottom lip. "I do need to check the new stiches, like I said." She kept her voice even, and her repetition was at a whisper.

Xander might have the balls to order a royal

around, but *she* didn't—even a former one. Funny, she'd never had the same qualms about the laird himself.

Maybe she wanted Alana to like her…because of Angus?

Oh, shut it, Lila.

She was *so* over herself this morning.

"Very well, but does he need to wake for such things?" Alana asked lightly.

"Alana." This time, Xander's voice was half-exasperation, half-growl. The man had spoken before Lila could comment.

She supposed she didn't need Alex awake to look at his leg, not *really*. Sleeping was keeping him from pain, right?

Duncan laughed. "Relax, brother. I dinnae believe his bonnie wife would do our laird any harm. No' truly."

Smugness settled over Alana's expression now that she had her brother-in-law's blessing.

Lila's conscience niggled at her. "Although, he'll need to eat. Soon."

"I'll see that he's awake by midday."

"If you do not, *I* will," Xander said, his voice full of threat, and promise.

Lila blew out a breath and shook her head as the family bicker continued, but Alana wasn't going to relent. There was no surprise where Angus had inherited his stubbornness. His smile graced her memory, and she banished their kiss from chasing it across her mind.

How long would he be gone?

She didn't have the guts to ask, and refused to acknowledge that she *might* miss him. Even just a little.

chapter twelve

Despite caring for Alex, and the daily patients who came to see Malcolm from around MacLeod lands, the days dragged on without Angus there.

Every morning her heart sank a bit more when he failed to appear at breakfast, and when someone remarked he and his cousins weren't back yet.

Lila wouldn't ask again of course, but someone — usually Claire or Alana always commented — as if to help put her out of her misery. As if they *knew* she was eager. Was dying to have information, hear his name spoken.

Finally, what felt like years later, instead of weeks, Iain burst into the laird's suite, shouting his brothers and cousin had returned, and the ladies all grinned and hurried out with the boy.

Lila swallowed and almost dropped her basket.

Alex didn't comment on her tarrying, but he asked if she was going to go, and she forced a nod.

"Tell my lad ta come see me," the laird said.

She offered another nod and retreated. Lila didn't go down to the hall. She took the back way to Malcolm's surgery, but her colleague wasn't in his domain. He was probably above, greeting the man she wanted to avoid.

The man who'd made her heart ache the longer he was gone.

Although Lila hated to admit it, she was miserable without him.

At some point, perhaps even before he'd kissed her that day outside of Malcolm's surgery, she'd started to care about Angus MacLeod, despite all the mental cautions and how much she knew better.

So, why wasn't she headed down to the great hall, where Angus' family was surrounding him, and Claire's two boys, no doubt demanding details of their journey?

If her discomfort would diminish by resting eyes on the man, she really *was* a fool. Lila was no doubt welcome in the great hall with the rest of the clan, but she couldn't make herself go. Maybe she was…afraid to see him? Afraid of what she'd do?

She scoffed. It wasn't like she'd throw her arms around him in public and lay one on him, even if she wanted to. She ignored the voice agreeing that was indeed a good plan.

Idiota. Estupida.

Lila busied her hands with tiding up after Malcolm. He'd left some jars out on one of the worktables, so she put them back in their assigned places, stacked a few baskets, and moved his mortar and pestle to its home near his apothecary drawers.

When there was nothing left to do, and the healer

still hadn't returned, she slunk to her room, taking the way she'd come so she wouldn't run into anyone. Every last MacLeod probably remained with Angus, Lan and Rory anyway.

She pushed into her room and wanted to throw herself on her bed. She could cry, but what good would that do?

She was responsible for her misery.

Lila *did* want to see him.

Something that wasn't there before caught her eye, so she went to the bedside table. Her hand shook when she picked up the small wooden box. She hadn't been in the surgery but maybe an hour. Somehow it didn't matter; instinct told her Angus had left the gift in her room.

It should bother her that he'd invaded her personal sanctum without permission, but Lila could almost scent sandalwood in the air, and her missing him was like a sharp dagger to her side.

Not seeing him for a whole fortnight had kicked her dreams into overdrive. She remembered his kiss as if it was yesterday. Her body wished for him like she didn't have the guts to do for real.

She'd been in the seventeenth century for a little over a month now, and Angus had been gone for almost half that time.

Absence makes the heart grow fonder. The old cliché tickled her mind. Lila didn't want to admit that was the case with Angus MacLeod, but it was true.

She *had* missed him over the last two weeks. Distracting herself with work only partially helped. Lila was overjoyed he was finally home.

There was a small piece of parchment on the table, with a messy scrawl of dark ink. It simply said, '*for you.*'

Simple, direct.

That was so Angus, wasn't it?

To the point, like when he'd told her he wanted her.

Lila almost didn't want to open it; it was small enough to contain jewelry, and why would he buy her that?

The little box was a work of art itself. A thistle and heather carved on the top in a repeating pattern, smaller around the lip. The design was intricate and beautiful, and in a rich dark wood, like Lila loved. The finish was shiny, too.

Had he known?

An unfamiliar girly gasp fell from her lips, and the present blurred in front of her eyes. Her necklace sat on a bed of black satin. A new chain gleamed in the candlelight in her room. Her tummy wobbled.

Lila opened the table drawer, where she'd put it for safekeeping. The small leather pouch Malcolm had given her was there, and of course it was empty.

Smart of Angus to leave it, because she'd checked for the pouch a few times, but had never peered inside, assuming her beloved piece of jewelry was tucked where she'd left it.

Looking now was silly, since it was before her, repaired and ready to wear. The new chain looked expensive, especially by seventeenth century standards.

The MacLeods weren't poor, but how had he afforded this?

The tear rolling down her cheek was followed by a few more. She wiped her face and admonished herself. She'd never been a crier. Her stomach was in knots — she was grateful and torn.

Lila took the necklace from the box and rubbed her thumb over the embossed surface of the Saint Luke medal like she'd done hundreds of times. She turned it over and inspected the caduceus. It had a sheen to it, as if just cleaned and polished.

She sniffled and smiled when the memory of it new in a much different kind of jewelry box surfaced in her mind. *"For you,* mija," *Lita* had said. *"So, you never forget your faith, and who healed others before you."*

"Faith, huh?" Lila whispered. She held the chain up. It was thicker than the fine white gold one that'd held her pendant originally, but somehow that meant more to her.

Her grandmother had bought it for her, but Angus had made it wearable again.

Lita had meant the world to her, but her Highlander taking the time to do this, when no one had asked…well, *that* meant the world to her, too.

Maybe…so did Angus.

She sniffled and wiped her face. Lila put the necklace around her neck. The new chain was longer, with Saint Luke now resting on her cleavage. She smirked. Somehow, she suspected Angus would appreciate that. She'd have to ask him.

Angus…

Lila needed to see him.

Right now.

She shut the bedside table drawer and whirled to the door. She rushed from the room and sprinted down the hall.

If he'd come upstairs, maybe he was done in the great hall. Lila prayed he was in his rooms.

She shoved the door open when he'd bid her to enter.

Angus stood by the trunk at the end of his large bed, and she'd caught him slipping a fresh shirt over his head.

Her heart skipped, and she wanted to ask him to take it back off. Only his abs had been visible, ridiculous abs unfair to the rest of mankind, and Lila wanted to see his whole body. Touch it, like she'd done in her dreams.

He'd told her he wanted her weeks ago.

Did he still?

Stop. What are you thinking?

Angus' hair was wet, and the sandalwood he'd always smelled like was thick in the air, even more alluring than normal. He'd obviously just bathed, and the scent of fresh peat hung in the room, too. He must've just renewed the fire in his hearth.

Lila rushed to him and threw her arms around him.

Angus was surprised, if his wide sapphire eyes were any indication, but it only took him seconds to pull her into his chest and even less time to meet her seeking lips.

She stood tiptoed to deepen the kiss, but opened her mouth when his tongue begged entrance, and quickly gave him control.

His hands were all over her back and ass, and Lila moved closer on a moan, already panting as her head spun and heart rebounded off her ribs.

He was hard, erection pressing into her belly, and she wanted to move closer, jump up and wrap her legs around his waist.

He wants me.

Could she be with him?

"Am I dreamin'?" Angus whispered against her mouth.

The haze of passion clouding Lila's head cleared slightly, but she didn't want him to talk; she wanted to keep kissing him.

Mentioning dreams made the demand of desire worse, the throb between her legs more intense; it made her think of how many times she'd woken achy and empty because her lover wasn't really in her bed.

Lila shook her head.

"Ye…ye…came ta me." He pulled back, and his very blue gaze raked her face.

"Thank you for my necklace." The blurt fell out, sounding distracted to her own ears. She wanted to demand his lips back on hers, but Lila's courage splintered.

The look in his eyes was wondrous, and…tender?

It was too serious, too scary.

She ordered herself to stop thinking. She touched the Saint Luke medal, and Angus looked where her fingers rested.

His eyes stayed on her breasts, and he licked his bottom lip, which already had a nice sheen, swollen from their kiss.

Awareness zinged down her spine, and Lila quivered against him. "I missed you," she confessed.

Angus' hold on her waist tightened.

Then there was a knock on his door.

The thick panel inched open before either of them said a word.

Lila flew from his arms as if he'd burned her, and her embarrassment screamed. Her face still seared, but arousal fled, and her stomach clenched as Alana entered the room. She averted her eyes and hoped like hell the woman didn't have a clue to what they'd been doing.

"Oh, Lila-lass, I'd no idea you were…here. We missed you down in the hall." The elegant lilt of her accent wrapped around Lila, but it didn't dissipate the heat from her face.

Alana sounded Scottish, of course, but her brogue wasn't rough like the burr of the MacLeods. She'd been born royal, after all, so her words were more enunciated and less rolled. Not less appealing, just different. Although, she'd been married a long time, and so every once in a while, she'd say a word like the others, in the same way Claire's accent had a mixed edge.

Her statement had been innocent, but Lila only felt accusation. She swallowed and straightened. Words fell from her mouth unbidden. "Angus fixed my necklace. I was…thanking him."

When her object of desire smirked, her cheeks scorched even more.

Lila couldn't look at him. Fingered her pendant. It helped her resist the compulsion to pace—or flee from the room.

His mother's smile was warm. "How wonderful."

Angus went to her, and somehow Lila could feel his missing heat, although they hadn't been touching.

Her body mourned.

She cursed herself.

"Thank ye fer comin ta say goodnight, Mother. Sorry I was too tired ta sup in tha hall." He dipped down to kiss Alana's cheek.

Her smile widened. "You're welcome, love, but I

came to get you."

"Oh?"

"Your father would like a word."

"Oh, a' course."

They shared a few more sentences, and Lila could only watch.

Alana's body language was normal, open, friendly, and loving toward her son, like always. She barely spared her a glance, but Lila *felt* judged regardless.

She wanted to excuse herself but didn't want to be rude.

Angus cleared his throat. "Ah, g'night, Lila."

"Thanks for my necklace." She fisted the new chain and tried not to cringe. She'd blurted again. It seemed to be a new talent—one she could do without. Besides, Lila had already thanked him, with words *and* a kiss, so there was no need to repeat herself.

Estupida.

He smiled, and it made her insides wobble. "Yer welcome."

Then he was gone.

Alana threw her a knowing smile, then followed her son.

Lila stood there. A voice whispered in the back of her mind to get in his bed. That she needed to wait for him—she ignored it.

"He didn't say it back." Her voice startled her, but she used the poor excuse to command her feet to take her back to her own room.

She tried to convince herself she wasn't bothered that Angus hadn't said he'd missed her, too.

chapter thirteen

eavy hands cupped her breasts from behind, kneading, squeezing, but the pleasure-pain only made her want more. Lila writhed against him, wiggling her ass against his erection. Hopefully he'd push inside her; and if not soon enough, she was going to combust.

Her eyes flew open, and the grip, the imagined heat, *poofed* from her body—from her bed.

She flipped to her back with a sigh that sounded ragged even to her own ears. Sweat beaded her brow and Lila was too warm for the comforter covering her, so she kicked it away, frowning. Her frown only deepened when she didn't see the gown she'd donned before sleep. She'd woken naked.

Again.

A glance to the right revealed the soft chemise was on the floor next to the bed—bright white in the absence of adequate light—but Lila didn't muster energy to retrieve it.

The throb between her legs was annoying. Perhaps even more so than the stupid dreams. That'd been the twentieth. Thirtieth? More than that? Maybe she'd suppressed the real number, so she didn't have to face it.

She'd dreamt of him so much it was embarrassing. During the two days he'd been back from Inverness, Lila could barely look him in the face without blushing like a fool. That was as much because *she'd* kissed *him* as much as from the fantasies.

Like the other dreams, this one didn't confirm his identity, but it didn't matter if she hadn't seen her lover's face in every vision — or any of them.

Angus.

It was *his* touch she moved into. His kiss she couldn't live without. His body she craved on top of hers. Holding hers. Behind hers. Hovering over hers.

Position didn't matter as long as he slid inside her.

Lila ran her hands over her breasts and down her stomach. Her skin was damp, sweat bathing her whole form as if he'd really been in her bed.

She kept her hand moving, touching her pulsing tender flesh. Her clit was swollen, ready. Her folds were wet, her sex begging for a man she'd denied. Declared she didn't want him, even though *that* was probably the biggest lie of her life.

Lila wanted him more than she'd ever wanted a man.

In the dreams, Angus had kissed her like he had in the corridor, and like she'd kissed him in his room the other night — which made sense since those were her memory's reference points. Damn, when Lila was asleep it was sharper than when she contemplated his mouth on hers in waking hours.

She did.

All. The. Time.

No matter how many times she banished Angus and his wicked mouth from her brain, it came back with a vengeance—especially since she had a fresh experience to draw from.

The lady doth protest too much.

"Yeah, well you can suck it, Shakespeare." Lila punched the mattress on either side of her naked body. She wasn't cold yet, so she left the blanket and sheet where they were, and crushed her eyes shut.

She was genuinely grateful he'd replaced the chain on her necklace—always would be. The jewelry graced her neck even now, but she *never* should've lost her head and gone to him.

Never should've kissed him. It'd just made the dreams worse, more real. Basically, she was torturing herself in her sleep.

Every. Damn. Night.

What am I going to do?

Sure, Lila could sleep with him. He wanted her; wouldn't reject her like she had him.

Angus hadn't called her on the unfinished business her kiss had left them with, and she could've hugged his mother for interrupting them. Alana had saved her from having to…what?

Sleep with him that night?

Her body sure as hell had wanted to. Still did.

Lila *shouldn't* sleep with him, even if it might escort her stupid dreams to hell where they belonged.

Lizzie was always telling her she needed to relax in that English accent of hers, but Lila hadn't "relaxed" with a man since before her fellowship had started.

When was the last time she'd had sex?

It'd been a quickie with a doctor from her home hospital in Dallas. They'd slept together a few times, but never more than a mechanical-relieving-stress kind-of-thing.

She couldn't even call him a lover. Dillon had made certain she got off, sure, but he hadn't touched her like Angus did in her dreams.

Like he would for real if she'd let him.

Lila shivered, but still wasn't affected by the drafty guest room. She hadn't had an actual lover for…years.

Could she go there with Angus?

The door to her room shut with a quiet *thud* and Lila jumped, yanking the comforter up to her chin.

The figure coming toward her was hidden in shadows thrown by a glowing candle so she couldn't see his face, but she didn't need to. Awareness darted all over her body before Lila could see his blue eyes over the ambient light of the small oil lamp—not candle—in his large grip.

Those hands…

Stop it. Dreams. Are. Not. Real.

Of course, she'd known his touch a few times in reality, when they'd kissed. Even through layers of material, Angus' touch had burned her flesh…maybe her soul.

Right, that's just ridiculous.

"Lass?" His deep voice was hesitant in a way she'd never heard from him.

Like Angus was afraid Lila might scream and announce his invasion to the castle. Or…kick his ass for coming into her room in the middle of the night.

Uninvited.

However,…she remembered a part of his magic was visions, premonitions, if she believed in that. Despite the fact she sat in a bed at Castle Dunvegan, in the year 1692, all the magic stuff was a lot to absorb without question.

Could he…*know* she'd been dreaming of him?

Lila startled and tremors chased each other down her spine. She swallowed. "Angus."

He didn't answer, but stopped within a foot of her bed, holding the lantern up so they could see each other.

She could touch him if she reached out. Lila was still overheated. Still aching with want, so the blanket was too hot, but she didn't dare shove it off. She was naked.

It didn't matter he'd seen her birthday suit on the beach. It didn't matter she was a doctor and not ashamed of any body, let alone her own.

She couldn't go through with her fantasies.

Admitting she *had* them was bad enough.

Lila compromised by sliding her arms on top of the fluffy MacLeod-tartan comforter.

Angus set the oil lamp on the bedside table, and the light bathed the room with a soft glow that carried to the end of the bed. His eyes tracked her movements. "Ye...ye dinnae wear anathin'?" His Adam's apple bobbed.

She straightened and perched her shoulders against the carved headboard, making sure the thick blanket covered her breasts, then cleared her throat. "I had a gown on when I went to sleep, but I...woke up naked." Her neck heated when she processed what'd just fallen out of her mouth, but since she'd arrived, Lila had never been able to lie to him—except when she'd decreed, she didn't want him.

Other than that, Angus scrambled her brain like she was a pining teenager, and her blurting was becoming world-famous—or maybe just seventeenth-century-Dunvegan-famous.

She growled at herself. "I guess I was hot."

The addition made his eyes shoot to her mouth and she cursed herself.

'*Hot*' and '*naked*' were not words to be used *to* Angus MacLeod.

Not out loud anyways.

"What do you want?" Lila tried to demand, but the question didn't come out hard enough.

Again, he studied her, so she kicked herself and added *'want'* to the do-not-speak list.

Please don't say me. Don't. Say. It.

She didn't trust herself to refuse him when she was unclothed, and he *could* be in a New York minute.

Angus only wore a long sleeping shirt, which hung to his knees. No usual kilt was in sight, and she'd bet her favorite stethoscope he had *nothing* on beneath it.

His feet were bare as well, so he'd truly come from his bed.

Maybe he does *know I was dreaming of him.*

Was her subconscious calling to him?

Lila fought a shudder but couldn't look away from his face.

He was so handsome it took her breath, even with the overnight stubble and his dark, mussed hair.

Maybe Angus was even more tempting unkempt, showing he wasn't so perfect. Not always put together in his Highlander staples.

"I dinnae ken what ta say; if I speak true, ye dinnae like tha answer."

Her heart stuttered.

He wants to say me. And wants me to be okay with it. Am I?

"What woke you?" she asked instead of acknowledging what she couldn't.

His gaze took on an intense edge. "I was dreamin' a' ye an' I..."

"Couldn't take it anymore." Her stomach prolapsed when she comprehended the statements — hers *and* his. Her cheeks scorched.

Angus stilled, but his fingers twitched like he wanted to reach for her and didn't dare.

Lila sucked in a breath, then another, but it failed to chase away the haze in her head or the desire thundering through her blood. She swallowed again and pushed to her knees on the edge of the bed, letting the blanket fall where it would.

Her Highlander's eyes went wide, and he didn't move, as if he thought her a vision that would disappear if he tried to come to her.

Part of her brain screamed, *what're you doing?*

The other part told good sense to go to hell, and Lila gestured to him. "I was dreaming of you, too. I have been. For weeks."

Angus stepped closer, his legs bumping into the bed, but he didn't touch her. His Adam's apple jumped for the second time, and she wanted to kiss his throat, among other places.

"What...wha' did yer dreams..." His voice cut off on a croak, like he couldn't get enough air to finish.

"You. Me. Naked."

His chest rose slightly, like Angus held his breath. "An'?"

"Kisses. Touches." Lila forced air into her lungs, to make herself keep talking. "You inside me."

He groaned, and his arms shot around her,

molding her to his chest.

She resented the fabric between them. Meeting his mouth halfway, her lips sought his, her tongue rubbing his, and her hands on a mission to fuse his skin to hers.

Lila yanked on his shirt, and her dream lover broke the kiss only to shuck it. Wrinkled fabric landed at his feet, discarded without further care.

Angus stood back for moments that felt like hours.

She needed to touch him, but she was grateful for the lantern. The light gave her a chance to survey him.

Her Highlander had seen her naked, but she'd never gotten the pleasure—and he was certainly *pleasing* to look at. *Gorgeous* — no surprise there.

Angus had a warrior's *body*; all sculpted muscles and defined lines. She wanted to run her fingers through the light dusting of dark curls on his chest and taste every inch of his eight-pack.

Speaking of inches…

His cock jutted toward her as if it approved of Lila's perusal, or perhaps it was begging like *she* wanted to. Angus' thighs were thick and even his calves were perfectly formed. The smattering of hair covering them complemented.

She bit her lip to keep from promising to lick *all* of him. Women in his century weren't supposed to be the forward ones.

Angus returned to her, holding her against his

chest.

Heat exploded. Lila's whole body thrummed.

He felt like she'd *known* he would, his flesh firm where she was soft.

Dream blurred with reality as he gently tipped them back so he could join her on the bed. His knee landed between her legs and Lila stared up at him as he held himself above her—the same as so many of her nightly fantasies.

Their eyes locked and her whole form vibrated with the command of his gaze. Instinct shouted what he was looking for. Affirmation; confirmation. He wanted to make sure she was okay, too.

Sure, about *him*.

"Yes, Angus."

He didn't move after her whisper; those incredible eyes assessed her. "Be certain, lass. Once I have ye, I dinnae let ye go."

Lila's heart thumped and she inhaled. Her senses swirled with sandalwood and arousal. She couldn't— *wouldn't*—argue with him about needing to go home—sex wouldn't change that.

She wanted him.

The selfish part of her didn't care about the rest. Not right now, anyway. "Kiss me. Touch me. Be with me. Please."

His mouth came back to hers on a mutual groan, then Angus kissed her into oblivion, making her doubt she *wasn't* dreaming. Their tongues danced and intertwined.

Lila clung to him, snaking her arms around him, and urging him to lower himself on top of her. When his pecs touched her breasts, his erection burned her thigh, and her sex answered with a demanding pulse.

As much as she wanted to explore him, she needed him inside her. The empty ache was enough to make her squirm.

"Fergive me, but I dinnae be able ta wait. I…need ye."

She lifted her pelvis and bumped his, rocking into him. Couldn't find the words to tell him that was fine. More than fine; Lila craved it.

They both moaned, and his massive chest pushed into her breasts. If it was possible, her nipples strained more, throbbing from the contact that was too much, and not enough.

Angus put his forehead on hers, and their collective pants echoed in her ears. "I want ta worship ye, Lila."

She shivered, like she always did when he said her name. Lila lifted her head from the pillow and nibbled his bottom lip. "Later."

His biceps tremored as he hovered above her. His gaze didn't waiver.

"Angus…" His name fell from her lips as a pleading whine. "Inside me." The order was too shaky, but at least she'd gotten it out. "Please. I…need you, too."

Angus groaned and kissed her again, his hand shooting between them. Clever fingers caressed her clit, and she whimpered.

Lila shifted beneath him; her sex throbbed, then clenched as if she couldn't survive the emptiness one second longer, but he put her out of her misery soon enough.

His tip nudged, then pushed forward, but it was gradual, inch-by-inch, as if she would shatter.

She broke the seal of their mouths.

Angus' handsome face was lined with his efforts to control himself.

Lila didn't want him reined in. She wanted her Highlander wild. Free. She wanted *all* of Angus MacLeod. "Angus. Take me hard. I won't break. I promise you."

He obeyed on a grunt, shoving forward to the hilt, seated deep inside her.

She shuddered as pleasure spread low and hot. She was so full, and it was so...*perfect*.

When he didn't move, she squeezed his arms and lifted her hips, begging without words.

Angus started to thrust without comment.

She ran her hands down his back, mapped his broad shoulders and muscled back. Lila followed his flesh lower, palming the globes of his very nice ass and holding on when he picked up speed. She kneaded him, encouraging, rocking, and moving under him as they found a natural rhythm.

His mouth took hers yet again, and she kissed him back with the same vigor of his lunges in and out.

Every nerve ending was alive, every inch of her body engulfed in a fire made of Angus-ecstasy. Everywhere he touched her, from the brushes of his fingers, to where their legs entwined, and his heaving chest rubbed her breasts, more pleasure traveled, as if coming from his pores and filling hers.

Lila had never felt someone so *completely.*

Pressure built slow and steady with every drive forward, until her inner muscles quivered, and she writhed, lifting her hips again; she was so close.

Angus surged into her over and over, answering her silent plea.

Her orgasm crested, and she broke their kiss to scream his name. Her arms and legs stiffened of their own accord, but so did her lover.

He stilled above her and tossed his head back, making his hair fly. Angus closed his eyes and whispered her name as her sex clenched and released around his, milking him.

The warm rush of his climax made her tremble, but all her muscles were doing the same, so it was just one more piece of intensity to process.

"Lila-lass." His soft voice broke the spell of watching him in his pleasure.

If it was possible, Angus was *beautiful* in that moment, even more gorgeous than before, if Lila could refer to a man as such, let alone the best lover she'd had in her life.

She shuddered again and swallowed. Twice.

Sapphire orbs locked onto hers, and she couldn't move.

He really is perfect.

"Are ye well? I dinnae hurt ye?" Angus froze, concern marring the orgasm afterglow.

"I'm…fine. Kiss me, Angus."

He flashed a smile that made her heart skip and obeyed, but it wasn't like the ones full of hungry passion when they'd made love.

It was a soft brush of his lips on hers, but he came back for more, as if he couldn't help himself, and gently entered her mouth, seeking her tongue with his.

His softening erection slipped from her body at the same time, but somehow the tenderness of his kiss made Lila feel less empty. Cherished, like when he lowered himself to the bed and gathered her against him.

Alarm bells sounded in her head.

This was supposed to be about sex, not cuddling a tender lover.

Sex.

Not making love.

It wasn't supposed to change anything. It was supposed to answer the call of rushing blood and unrequited desire.

Push him away, Lila. He doesn't need to hold you.

"I need ta hold ye," Angus said, as if he'd heard her thought and rejected it.

Her body went lax against her will, and Lila nestled into him, shooting her arms around him like she had the right.

Like she owned him.

Rightness settled over her.

Scared the shit out of her.

Tell him to leave.

Her heart skipped, then sped up as if it hadn't worked hard enough moments before, when they'd made love.

Stop saying that. It was just sex.

Sex. Sex. Sex.

Lila pulled back to look at his face, but Angus was reclined in her bed, eyes closed. Looking relaxed and satisfied. His elbow was bent, hand tucked behind his head, and his breathing settled into a normal rhythm. His cheeks were still flushed from exertion, but his mouth had the corners turned up.

He was *still* beautiful.

It didn't feel like just sex.

As if he could sense she was staring, those gorgeous blue eyes opened, and he flashed a lazy, sated smile.

Somehow, it made her insides ripple.

His skin held a sheen of sweat, but that only made Lila fantasize about licking his chest to taste the salt. Hollering at herself didn't diminish the desire, especially when he peered at her with much the same fascination.

"I've ne'er seen a more bonnie lass." Angus snagged an arm around her waist, settling a large hand on her lower back and urging her to return to him.

She didn't fight him.

Maybe she *couldn't*.

Lila rested her cheek on his chest as his fingers started walking soothing circles on her damp skin, and she relaxed into his body on a sigh.

Whether contentment or resignation, she didn't want to explore, but she couldn't pull away from him. Not at the moment, anyway.

She let the even *thump-thump* of his heart and the steady caress on her back drift her off to sleep.

chapter fourteen

e'd been coming to her room nightly, and Lila couldn't refuse him. Angus was the best lover she'd ever had. He could make her body sing.

It was almost as if he could get inside her head. Or instinct guided his hands. He knew where and how she wanted to be touched without a word passing her lips.

Damn, the man could kiss. Lit her on fire with the barest touch—of his anything on her anything.

A voice whispered there was more to it than just the physical, and of course Lila pushed it away. She couldn't handle the feels where her Highlander was concerned.

She was going home, and *that* was all there was to it.

Unprotected sex wasn't something she'd done much, if ever. Although she'd never cared for condoms, she'd always used them. However, even if they'd been easily available in this time and she could use them, Lila couldn't imagine bearing that separation with Angus.

If she recalled correctly, some form of a condom dated back to the fifteenth century, but she wasn't about to investigate if anyone had any—didn't want to imagine what it'd be made of. Some animal bladder or intestine, no doubt. Not sanitary for sure.

Besides, she wanted nothing between her and Angus, except skin, sweat and a lot of heat.

She didn't have to worry about pregnancy, because her birth control implant was good for several more months. She'd gotten it from her OBGYN at her hospital in the US, long before her fellowship had started.

Lila ran her fingertips over the bump on her arm. It wasn't visible by sight, but she could feel it beneath the surface of her skin. When the time came, if she had to remove it herself, she could, but there would be no replacement in the seventeenth century.

There were natural herbs to prevent unwanted conception, but she wasn't sold on them completely. There were no ninety-nine percent guarantees like with her contraceptive.

Perhaps she could subtly ask Malcolm, but it wasn't something she wanted to contemplate. The healer would no doubt wonder why Lila was inquiring—even if he didn't come out and ask. Could she blame it on a shy female patient?

Selfishly, she didn't think she could or would stop sleeping with her Highlander, so she'd put off concerns until she had to deal with them.

In another month, likely her patient would be walking. Alex was healing quite nicely. So it was probably a non-issue.

Lila would be back to modern-day Scotland by the time her implant needed to be replaced.

Angus would always sneak out of her suite before sunrise, as if they both weren't consenting adults, but she understood his need to save face for the sake of his family.

She already adored the MacLeods, but she understood that they could be a smothering lot. If they were caught, she envisioned the razzing his uncles would provide. Teasing aside, premarital sex was a no-no for the century, but of course, men did what they wanted anyway.

Insert eyeroll.

At least with them on the down-low, Lila's reputation wasn't in question. Not that she cared, but she should. The last thing she needed was any of the MacLeod elders discovering she and Angus were lovers and having the *you-have-to-marry* issue pressed.

It just wasn't going to happen. Ever.

She could explain an unplanned child wouldn't be a concern, but that undoubtedly wouldn't matter. Impropriety was what it was, and discovery would come with expectations and consequences she'd rather not deal with.

During the day, when their paths crossed, Lila couldn't look at Angus without *feeling* him all over her—no matter the normal, respectful distance he always maintained, especially if she was checking on his dad.

Just being near him resulted in insta-arousal, as if he had some sex magic. No matter how much she ridiculed herself for being a giant hormone, nothing cured her. Their chemistry was incendiary.

She silently begged him to back her into a dark corridor and take her, but he never did. Kissed her a few times when no one was around, but Angus always backed off and promised he'd finish what they'd started at night. He'd never failed on that vow, either.

Lila watched the men on the fighting yard in the bailey every morning after her rounds with the laird. Without a shirt, her lover was impressive when he was performing swordplay or hand-to-hand combat.

She stood behind a wooden fence with the castle looming over her, offering shade in the bright sun. The light, warm breeze countered the cool spring morning.

The air was full of shouting and laughing men and the clashing of metal on metal. Sometimes the verbal content was reprobate, but she didn't care.

These men were warriors who protected their own. They were brothers, too, even if not all by blood. As tough as they were, they loved just as hard.

That was a sight to behold. Lila had never thought she'd be attracted to such possessiveness, but it did make a girl feel wanted.

The women were busy with their day-to-day, but Alana and Claire insisted Alex remain her priority, so she was always turned away when she'd offered to help with chores. They relegated her to Malcolm and his surgery, and *Lita* would be proud of all she'd learned.

She'd spent a few hours with Angus' little sister, Lexi. The girl was sweet but stubborn, and of course, like most young women, felt repressed by her family. Lila laughed; that plight didn't seem to change, no matter the century.

Lexi had apologized multiple times for Lila being sucked back in time, but she wasn't upset, and had told her so. She had a purpose here — and a lover.

Lila didn't regret her circumstances, but she did worry over what was going on at the hospital and with her friends, despite the note Xander had already promised had been delivered. Lizzie and Sophie would worry. Probably think the letter was an indication she'd gone crazy, especially since they wouldn't find her, no matter how extensive the search. There still remained no logical explanation of her disappearance. Contemplating the magic of it all hurt her head, so she tried to let it go until it was time.

The men didn't take it easy on each other, even the teenagers, Angus' cousins. There'd been a few heart-stopping moments, but her Highlander had never been seriously hurt, and he'd always taken revenge on the man who'd put him on his back, especially if it'd been one of his uncles. The boys were the same, fierce with their swords.

Little Iain, at age ten, was just beginning his lessons with his father and Xander, but Angus taught him as well, and Lila loved seeing their interactions.

Her lover was patient but firm with the little guy. A part of her loved that the big strong warrior was good with kids. *That* forbidden part resurfaced, and teased her mind with things that could never be. Things she didn't want anyway.

Right?

Back to the feels I don't need.

What she had with Angus was temporary. She needed to pin that to her brain.

Emotions weren't an option. The sex was awesome, but it was just physical, like when she'd been with Dillon. Only for release.

Lila couldn't accept anything else.

Be a hardass surgeon.

Awareness that someone was watching her prickled the back of her neck, and she swung her head around. Her gaze collided with Alana's.

Angus' mother smiled, it was sweet and genuine, but somehow made Lila flush. Instinct told her the woman knew what she'd been doing with her son.

Lila tried not to gulp as the ethereal beauty approached. The former princess wore a pretty, simple gown. The bodice was striped with two different hues of purple, the only color she'd seen her wear since she'd arrived. Of course, the skirt billowed, flowing as she walked, like she was floating.

Didn't that just go with her persona?

It was hard to believe she was in her seventies. Alana didn't look any older than her husband — if that.

Her fair hair showed no signs of graying and was swept up in a simple knot at the back of her neck. Regality clung to her; despite the fact she'd fled her realm to be with Alex. She was the laird's wife, but she'd been born to be a queen.

Alana had said she regretted nothing — except that it'd taken her too many years to be with her family. She hadn't been able to escape the Fae Realm until Angus was nine, as the story went. He'd been with the MacLeods, raised away from his mother.

How sad was that?

He didn't seem to suffer from it, but he *was* almost thirty. His sister had never shared his fate; since their mother had been in the Human Realm by the time Lexi had come along.

Their family was so tightknit, finding out things had started out rocky for Alex and Alana had been a shocker.

Seeing that *they* had a happily-ever-after just made Lila's gut churn more. She didn't need ideas — even ones she promptly denied.

"Good day."

She inclined her head and tried to relax. It wasn't like the woman was going to jump on her. Or challenge her to a duel. "Mornin'."

"You almost sounded Scottish." Alana's smile

widened to a grin.

Lila let out a breath and hoped to hell Angus' mother couldn't sense her nerves. Then she remembered the laird's wife had magic that could let her *feel* other people's emotions. She tried not to cringe.

"Are you well, lass?" Her voice was light with a cautious edge—as if Alana was wondering if Lila would lie to her.

Lila cleared her throat. "Aye." The Scottish word rolled off her tongue without thought.

Alana smiled again. "Some things tend to grow on a person."

She means Angus.

The woman didn't need to call her out directly. She was employing psychological warfare like only a mother could. The subtlety was as plain as if she'd said, *'What are your intentions with my son?'*

"Sorry, I tend to pick up the vocabulary of those around me. *'Aye'* here is kinda like *'y'all'* in Texas. I've been in Scotland a year in my time..." Lila shrugged and swallowed. She'd sounded nervous to her own ears and fought a bad case of the fidgets.

"Ah. A word my sister-by-marriage is fond of."

"It blows my mind that Claire is from Texas. Then her sister's here, too..."

"As she would say, 'tis a small world."

Lila felt her shoulders loosen with every sentence Alana spoke. At least Angus' mother was easy to talk to. She let out a small breath and let her eyes skip over the men again.

Her lover faced off against two men—one was his Uncle Duncan, and the other a fair-haired man she didn't know. He was giant, even taller, and broader than them. Older, probably around Duncan's age, with a thick reddish-blond beard, but age wasn't holding him back in the least.

Angus held his sword high and rushed them with a Gaelic battle cry.

The other men, including Duncan's three boys and Xander's son, surrounded the trio, offering encouragement and quips alike. They were betting, too, exchanging wagers and gestures as the fighters circled each other.

Her pulse echoed in her temples as anxiety and excitement rolled over her. Her Highlander was *good.* The huge weapon was like an extension of his arms. Angus definitely knew what he was doing with it. His movements were graceful, fluid as he sparred.

"I see how you watch him."

Tension tightened Lila's spine all over again, and her heart skipped.

What was she supposed to say to *that*?

Yeah, I watch him a hell of a lot closer when he's in my bed.

Something every mother wanted to hear about their kid, right?

Lila could deny it—say she was watching *all* the

men, but even if Angus' mother wasn't magical, she had good instincts. Plus, she was observant.

More than once, she'd felt Alana's eyes on them during normal interactions. She was sharp, and hadn't meant Lila was watching her son *only* now on the fighting yard.

Alana's hand on her arm made her jump. "'Tis…okay, as you and Claire would say."

"What?" she blurted.

The gorgeous woman looked out over the men, a soft smile on her face. "When he was a laddie, Angus would use magic if he was losing a sparring match. 'Twas amusing…at first. Then his father would chase him until he caught him and demand I help him get revenge with my powers."

Everyday talk of magic still caught her off-guard, but Lila gave Alana a smile she couldn't help, imagining Alex running after his son all over Dunvegan. She was glad the woman hadn't addressed her blurt.

Her heartbeat hadn't calmed, a clue that it was only a matter of time, but Lila would take any reprieve she could get. "What did you do?" Curiosity got the best of her.

The former princess' smile turned mischievous. "Got revenge on both of them, of course. Then they both chased *me*."

Lila laughed.

"He watches you, too."

She tried not to startle.

"It seems your draw to each other is mutual," Alana continued as if Lila hadn't had a knee-jerk reaction, but that was too much to hope for.

"What do you want me to say?" she whispered. She tried to avoid that violet stare, but couldn't make it stick.

Her lover's mother wore that same gentle smile. "You don't have to say a thing."

A sigh breached Lila's lips. "I have to go home. When Alex is better, I have to go, I can't stay here. I have two more years of my fellowship, and I worked my ass off for it. I..."

Sound selfish.

She couldn't add that, even though what she'd already said was more than she'd wanted to confess. The words kept tumbling out, as if Alana had used some kind of truth serum on her. "I can't get attached to him. I just...can't."

The curve of the older woman's mouth remained in place, but her eyes declared, '*it's already too late.*'

Lila shook her head, denying the unspoken. Emotions she wanted to ignore swirled around her mind, and her insides wobbled. Again, she wanted to avert her gaze from her lover's mother and failed. Her eyes smarted as if she might cry, and she ordered a shutdown on that. Slammed the vault door in her head.

You're stronger than this.

Moments of silence passed, unnerving her, notching up Lila's heartrate the longer the former princess declined to offer a response.

The din of the men was the only noise, but somehow, she couldn't look away from those knowing purple orbs.

Speak, she wanted to order, even though there was no doubt she'd hate anything Alana might have to say.

"Guard your heart, my lass."

Lila gulped. Actually gulped. Words evaporated, because she hadn't expected *that,* even if she couldn't have guessed how Angus' mother would answer.

Alana's expression was serene yet knowing. She inclined her head and whirled away.

Lila watched her disappear into Dunvegan, her stomach in knots.

chapter fifteen

He palmed her calf and dragged his hand upward, savoring her supple skin. Angus couldn't stop touching her, so he caressed her thigh and followed the curve of her perfect bottom. He kept going, stroking her lower back, and trailing two fingers up her spine. He traced her shoulder blades, then because he couldn't help himself, dipped down and kissed the back of her neck, lingering there, pushing forward to taste her earlobe.

Lila moaned and he paused, waiting to see if she would wake.

Angus lay on his side behind her, and the MacLeod quilt from her bed was bunched at the end, but still covered their feet. He kissed her neck again, moving his tongue in a little circle below her ear. This time he elicited a whimper and couldn't bite back his smile. "I'm sorry I woke ye," he whispered.

Lila peered over her shoulder with only one eye cracked open. "Liar."

He chuckled and touched her upper arm, because he still couldn't quite keep his hands off her.

His lass rolled toward him, and his gaze rested on her breasts on full, glorious display. Her nipples were peaked. Tempting. "Are ye cold?"

Lila shook her head. "How could I be cold with you laying beside me? You're like a human radiator."

Angus leaned down and brushed his mouth over hers.

She responded quickly, slipping her arms around him, and nestling closer. She kissed him back, and he pressed ever deeper, until they swapped control and their tongues dueled as much as danced.

His cock stood at attention, despite having had her already. He tried not to get lost in the desire and heat flaring up so he could taste her longer. Angus wanted her again with a fierceness that shocked and worried him.

He was *starved* for Lila.

Angus broke the kiss on a pant, studying her flushed cheeks and heavy-lidded eyes. "Yer so bonnie," he breathed.

Her mouth curved in an alluring little smile, but she pulled back and met his gaze. "And you're...braw."

Angus laughed again and squeezed her against him.

"What? Isn't that right?"

"It...works, as ye say."

Lila flashed another smile that made his gut quiver. She snuggled closer, tucking her head under his chin.

He tightened his arms around her, slipping into a sense of serenity as her breath tickled his neck. As much as he burned for her, to be inside her again, holding her was perfect, too. He'd never been with a woman who tossed him into such mixed emotions. Contradictions that seemed to…make sense.

As if they *were* fated, as his mother had said.

Even though he'd grown up with and around magic, that was a bit much, wasn't it?

Angus blinked and kissed the top of her head.

"Angus?"

"Aye, *mò gr*–" He almost choked on the endearment so it wouldn't exit his mouth. He couldn't call her his love, in Gaelic or English. It would make her pull away, and now he had her where he wanted her.

Angus wouldn't let her go.

Surely, she'd guess the meaning, if she didn't already *know*. It was a common enough sweet nothing, said many times over at Dunvegan. Lila *was* his love—whether she admitted that, or not.

Whether he could tell her or not.

Even though his little healer hadn't brought it up since they'd become lovers, she was still planning on going back to the future—as soon as she felt his da was well enough.

Angus' heart thumped and slid to his toes.

How could he survive her walking away?

I can't let her go.

"Hey, are you all right?" Lila put her hand on his chest and pushed until he loosened his grip. Her dark eyes raked his face, and she wore a frown.

"Aye. What were ye gonna say?"

"I was gonna ask why you suddenly stiffened, but then you…did you just choke?"

"Are ye askin' as a healer?" He shook his head, his hair tickling the back of his neck. "I'm hale."

Lila didn't answer and stared long enough to make him fight a fidget.

Angus cupped her cheeks and drew her back to him, covering her mouth with his. If he couldn't distract her with a half-truth, a kiss worked just as well. She'd always responded to that, even when she'd declared he hadn't had a right to kiss her and shoved him away that first time in the corridor outside Malcolm's surgery.

Even then…she kissed me back.

Like she was now, winding her tongue around his and clinging to him, her arms around his neck and fingers buried in his hair.

"Angus." Lila pushed his name into his lips on a wild breath. "I need you. I need you inside me again."

His pulse quickened at her wanton demand. "Then I shall have ta oblige, my lady." Angus' tease came out amongst heavy breaths, losing the jesting edge, but he didn't care, as long as he had her. His need ran as high as hers, his blood at a rolling boil.

He covered her body, but Lila opened for him, arms, and legs. Angus fell into her; her pelvis cradling his. He was welcome where he was, but not only that, he was *home* when she held him like this. His bollocks ached — as if he'd not climaxed just an hour before.

She cupped his stubbled cheek. "Are you worried about something? You look worried…"

He turned his face and kissed her palm, smiling slightly to return the soft one she wore. "Nay, lass. Yer s'posed ta be driven mad with passion, no' talkin' o'er serious things."

Lila giggled and patted his face. "Well, I guess you just need to do a better job of distracting me."

Angus grinned. "My pleasure, lass."

"Mmm…pleasure…that's a good word." She licked her lips and he barely held back a groan.

He dipped down to taste her again, deepening the kiss only seconds after taking her mouth, because like everything else with her, it wasn't enough otherwise. Angus stroked her breasts, thumbing her nipples before adding his mouth, then moving downward, until she writhed beside him.

"More," she whispered.

"Aye." He traced her stomach with his tongue, dragging licks and nips onto her navel and over the soft part of her belly.

Lila moaned and tossed her head back, making the glorious length of her ebony locks flutter. She buried her hands in his hair like earlier, but this time she tugged.

His scalp smarted, but he didn't give a shite. A sword in his back couldn't make him abandon his quest.

Angus parted her already slick folds with a gentle finger, but followed quickly with his tongue, laving the tight bundle of nerves at the top of her sex.

A cry melted into a whimper when he sucked her into his mouth, and she pulled harder on his hair.

He chuckled against her tender flesh, and she started to pant his name as if chanting a spell.

She lifted her hips and rocked into his face, until he held her to the bed with one heavy hand on her hip. He couldn't spare them both if he was to continue his exquisite torture.

"Annngggus." Lila's voice was just below a screech as her body begged him more than his name on her lips.

As he teased, a new rush of wet warmth seeped from her center, bathing his tongue and fingers. He reveled in her arousal. She was so wet, so ready for him. So sweet. He wanted her again, aye, to have her convulse against his cock, but he wanted *this* more.

"Patience, *mò gradh.*"

"Since…when…are…you…not…desperate?"

Angus' eyes found her face and his breath stalled, his new laugh dying before fully born. He didn't have time to contemplate the endearment that'd slipped out anyway. He was swept away in his lover's radiance.

Lila was gnawing on her kiss-swollen bottom lip, her tresses mussed on the pillow and surrounding her like a dark aura. Her cheeks flushed several delicious shades of pink, highlighting the gorgeous lines of her high cheekbones, and her wanton expression was likely to unman him.

Angus cleared his throat. "I *am* desperate fer ye. But I am so, fer taste as much as take."

She tilted her head back and released the most enticing moan when he punctuated his words with another lick to her sex.

Her soft walls pulsated around his finger, so he slid another inside her, slowly moving in and out as he swirled his tongue around her most sensitive spot.

"More." Lila panted the demand and he smiled against her folds.

"Aye, my lady." He nipped her tight bundle with his teeth and thrust his fingers faster.

She screamed her orgasm even before his hand felt it, but he lapped up the moisture, inhaling her passion as much as it coated his lips. Her uninhibited response was like the honey of her arousal and made his cock pound.

He'd never had a lover like his little healer. She was so free, so receptive and reactive to his touch, his kiss.

Would that she felt the same way about his heart.

Angus tried not to give in to his startle, but Lila was too blissed out as she sighed to notice that he'd jerked. Hopefully, she'd missed him calling her his love, as well.

She reached for him, tugging his forearms. Her movements were frantic as she tried to get closer, and she trailed kisses on the only skin she could reach—his chest and upper stomach.

He chuckled and cupped her face. "Did ye like tha', my Lila?"

Her smile was sated, but no less stirring. "Aye, my Highlander."

It was as good as any endearment because she'd implied possession.

Angus' gut quivered, and he needed a distraction so his feelings wouldn't tumble out. He dipped down and kissed her.

Lila responded quickly and fiercely like always, firing his blood all over.

He gasped into her mouth when she enclosed hot fingers around his erection.

She broke away. "I need this…*you*…inside me."

Angus swallowed and shuddered. "Aye."

Lila squeezed and stroked him from root to tip enough times to make his bollocks clench and threaten to blow his top.

He grabbed her hand and kissed her knuckles. "Ye keep doin' tha', an' ye'll have ta wait fer me ta grant yer wish."

The smile she flashed was unrepentant, but his love lay back and opened her arms. "Take me."

He covered her body with his again and didn't hesitate. One thrust forward joined them completely, and she gasped into his ear.

"Angus, God, I—"

She held him tighter as he drove forward, her words drifting off as he took her hard and fast, just like she liked.

He'd learned everything he'd needed to know about her body in their short time as lovers, and always gave her what she wanted.

Angus only wished he could say the same of her heart.

He called himself a fool and surrendered to the pleasure of her perfect sex gripping his like a glove, quivering around his plunges, giving clues that his little healer was close to another climax.

The bottom of his spine tingled, and his bollocks prickled, indicating he wasn't far behind.

He pulled out only to propel forward in a hard thrust that had ecstasy exploding behind his eyes. It shot down his back and into his limbs, leaving his muscles stiff as his erection jerked and he spilled himself inside her. Angus grunted and buried his face in her neck.

Her skin was damp—hell, they were both soaked with sweat, but he didn't care. He wanted to stay like this, with her, inside her, for the rest of his life.

For moments he didn't move, unsure he could, but he didn't want to crush Lila, either. When he went to shift off her, his love held him tight.

His stare shot to hers, as if compelled. Her eyes were so dark, so alluring. He couldn't look away.

"Angus?" Lila whispered.

"Aye?" He sucked *'mò gradh'* back, and it about killed him.

"Earlier, you called me something…" Her pretty face contorted as she seemed to struggle for her thought.

Angus' heart stuttered, but he prepped a quick denial and perched it on the end of his tongue.

"I think…you said, *'mò gradh'*. I've heard Duncan say it before. Claire said…" Lila took a breath that lifted her breasts into his chest.

Angus tried to ignore his sharp awareness that every inch of her body touched every inch of his. Depending on what she said next, and how he responded, it might be the last time he'd touch her like this.

If he confessed his feelings, she'd run.

"Claire said," she repeated. "It means, *'my love'*."

Her gaze appeared obsidian and pinned him where he lay, as good as being held at swordpoint.

chapter sixteen

Lila watched the panic dart across his face, and her big Highlander reddened to the tips of his ears — this time exertion from lovemaking wasn't the culprit.

It made Angus seem younger. Innocent?

An almost thirty-year-old man could blush?

Who knew?

He'd called her *'my love'*, in Gaelic.

Lila's gut shouted she was right — even though he looked as if he'd deny it.

Which was silly, right?

He wasn't stupid. Angus would *know* she could confirm with any Gaelic-speaking clanmate as soon as she stepped out that door.

In this case, she didn't need to. His uncle called his aunt the same all the time. As she'd told her lover, Claire had explained the meaning.

Wait. He called me…what?

Her heart tripped.

But why? reverberated in her mind.

Not to question the use of the endearment, but to *interrogate* her body's reaction to the idea of Angus considering her *his love*.

Why did Lila's heart pound, her stomach quiver? Her head felt heavy.

Am I happy?

Calling her his love wasn't the same as if Angus had said the three little words starring one that started with an *L*. It would be in the middle, the brilliant center, and it was *absolutely* forbidden.

Just...*couldn't* happen.

Lila's pulse thundered in her temples.

Falling for him had always been a bad idea, but the notion that he might've...fallen for *her*...

Is it better or worse?

Examining the inside of her head didn't offer clarity, and Angus was still staring at her with wide sapphire eyes and crimson cheeks like a boy half his age — like one of his cousins.

Discomfort, and perhaps a little fear, made her stomach flip again, in the wrong direction. Lila fidgeted against his warm body as the urge to slip from the bed and retreat demanded her focus. She caught her eyes scanning the suite for...an escape?

Where would she go?

Besides, they were in *her* room. If anyone was going to leave, it should be *him*.

Could she ask him to go?

Order it?

How could she be rude to the man who rocked her world every time they were together? Two weeks that felt like months...years?

Angus pleased her without effort. Made her body hum and crave his touch. Made her come like no man ever had before.

But…it's not supposed to be about feelings.

Let alone *love.*

Lila shuddered. She crushed her eyes shut, took a breath and gathered the balls to look him in those eyes again. Fought the drive to crumble against him and forget this whole *'my love'* thing. Beg him to take her again. Make *love* to her again.

God, stop it. Now.

"Angus…"

His Adam's apple bobbed. "Aye?"

"I think you should leave."

Surprise darted across his face before his expression fell. Visible hurt dominated, and he averted his gaze.

Her heart slid to her toes, but she made herself break their physical contact. She gathered the sheet against her, hiding her nudity, and stood from the bed.

Angus didn't move. Didn't look at her, either.

"Please," Lila whispered, praying her word was steady. So many things played on her tongue, but she didn't know where to start.

Perhaps, she shouldn't. It'd never been a secret that she intended to go home. There was no need to remind him of that, right?

Why did the idea feel *wrong* suddenly?

Nausea skirted Lila's already twisted gut. She swallowed and tried not to stare at the lover she'd just obviously crushed. She jumped when he finally glanced in her direction.

Angus pinned her with his very blue eyes, and the intensity there matched his suddenly tight jaw and clenched fists. His massive chest heaved with an audible breath.

She forbade herself from watching the play of his muscles.

"I'll leave, if ye wish it. *Fer now.*"

"For now?" The two words weren't smooth. Her question had been interrupted with a choked gulp of air — the only thing that kept her from throwing up on her bare feet.

"Aye." His nod was definitive. "I vowed ta ye I'd no' let ye go, and I've nay intention of doin' so."

Lila's heart leapt — or maybe just skipped again, enough to add dizziness to the churning in her head and tummy. She clutched the sheet to her neck, even though she wanted to grab her middle and double over. There was really no use in hiding her body. He'd seen it all. Touched it all. Tasted it all. "Angus —"

"I tol' ye, lass. Once I had ye, I dinnae plan on lettin' ye go. Nothin's changed." His repetition made her far worse, and she wobbled on her feet.

Angus swept from her bed, grabbed his clothes and was gone before his vow had completely processed in her ears. Her Highlander didn't even pause to get dressed.

Lila ignored how her vision blurred and her whole form ached. She dashed to the bed and threw herself down, calling herself every name she could think of, in English, Spanish, and even the Gaelic word for *fool*, that Lachlan had taught her.

When the tears came, scorching her cheeks, she didn't try to stop them, but she couldn't quite put her finger on *why* she was such a mess.

She'd kicked Angus out, after all.

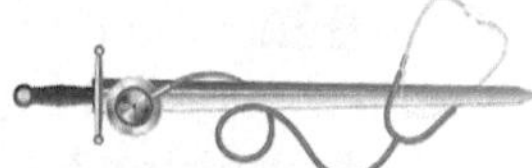

"I think you should leave." His little healer's words reverberated in his mind as Angus stumbled to his room. His whole body bled agony. Every inch of him hurt.

A sharp pain on his right side grabbed his attention, and he knocked his shoulder into the wall, in lieu of falling over. The rough surface made his bare biceps throb, but he pushed off and grabbed his gut.

He'd probably end up with a scrape on his upper arm. More unfortunate than the small would-be scratch, applying pressure around his waist didn't help.

After a few deep breaths, Angus forced his feet to move. He'd not want to be found in the corridor, holding his clothing over his tender bits, with a very bare arse.

Questions would never be welcomed, but now

that Lila had torn his heart out, it was even worse.

Angus wrenched his room open, and slipped inside, closing the door as quietly as he could manage. He dropped his clothing, and collapsed on his bed, staring up at the ceiling he couldn't see anyway, since the room was so dark. Cold, too, like the place where he used to have a warm organ that beat for a healer who…didn't want him.

"Nay." His whisper made his limbs shake.

Lila *did* want him—physically anyway, his sex inside hers. Just not the thing she'd torn from his chest and shattered when she'd ordered him from her bed.

Why hadn't he said anything?

Because she'd caught him, like a lad in mischief, with the endearment on his tongue and Angus hadn't known *what* to say. Would've likely blurted something he couldn't take back. Something that would've made her pull even further away.

He might've bared the heart she wanted nothing to do with.

It wouldn't have gotten me anywhere.

He bit back a groan and rolled over, clutching his side. It was still killing him. When that didn't lessen the pain, he reverted to his back, which seemed to make the discomfort release to a dull ache this time. At least for the moment.

What had Lila done to him?

A cracked laugh made its way out, but that made him hurt worse—not his heart, his side. Very real, actual pain.

Angus made a fist and punched the offending spot, but that only made him grapple for air as true agony jolted outward, as if trying to dagger his fist to get revenge.

He shot to a sitting position and coughed. The jarring movement only aggravated the tightness there, and he clutched himself again, ordering his lungs to take in air.

Angus told himself to breathe in the rhythmic pattern that he'd always used when he'd gotten the wind knocked out of him on the fighting yard.

Had he hurt himself training that morning?

He'd traversed the rest of the day with no issue, and certainly hadn't had any discomfort when he'd taken Lila after supper. Twice.

Had the little healer cursed him?

Laughing again hurt, and Angus shook his head. She'd cursed him all right; her words had pierced him as sure as a poisoned sword.

It'd been *his* mistake. He'd called her, '*mò gradh*' and his suspicions that she knew the phrase's meaning had been correct. She'd shut down—shut him out, as he'd feared.

If he'd known what she would do, why did it *hurt* so badly?

Because the little healer had been the owner of his heart for some time, whether she knew it or not.

"I love her." The whisper grated on his ears, but

it was true, nonetheless. Angus had fallen in love with Lila.

When, he couldn't recall. It was as if it'd always been. Maybe it'd happened the first day he'd lain eyes on her, naked and disoriented on the beach.

Fate?

He blew out a breath and cursed his mother's stupid notions.

They'd had a rough beginning, and now a rough…ending, so it couldn't be.

Angus choked on another breath, this one startled. He *refused* to believe he and Lila were done. He'd declared to her—twice—before his retreat that he wasn't going to let her go.

If that was true…

"How?" he whispered.

How was he going to get her back?

He threw his legs over the side of his bed and stood slowly. The pain in his side loosened, if only a little. Perhaps he should go see Malcolm, but it was late, and he wasn't dying.

Was he?

Not from whatever ailed his body.

Maybe Angus had taken a hit he couldn't recall right now. Duncan and the lads had group-attacked him, but he'd given as much as he'd taken.

He looked down, but the room didn't hold much light, since his hearth had already been banked. From what he could tell, his right side appeared normal—

there was no visible bruising or swelling. Even in the dimness he'd see that, right?

His fingers probed gently. Angus could start a fire to see better—or even use some candles; or the lantern on his bedside table—but didn't have the desire.

He hissed when pressure from his own touch offended whatever was wrong. His right side was made of agony that only worsened when he tried to walk.

Walk. One in front of the other. Breathe and it will go away.

He wasn't a laddie. Could take some pain. Angus stumbled to the table in his room, wincing as he went. The short distance shouldn't have been a feat, but he panted all the way there. His hands landed heavily on the back of the closest chair, and he had to convince his lungs to expand again by repeating his fighting mantra.

He'd taken a meal in his room the day before, and there was a pitcher of ale left. He'd not permitted any of the servants to come in and tidy up.

Angus didn't bother to pour himself a tankard. He grabbed the large thing and brought it to his lips, making a face when the warm liquid hit his tongue and burned down his throat. The quantity was enough to do the job.

He made it back to his bed and plopped down with more vigor than the wooden frame liked, if the loud squeak was any indication. His side didn't like that either, and throbbed a protest.

Somehow, he'd managed not to spill his drink, which was handy. He glanced at the pitcher and took another swig.

Then he proceeded to do what any respectable man with a broken heart did; get piss drunk.

Maybe when Angus passed out, the pain would stop.

chapter seventeen

"**A**ngus, wake, love." The voice was familiar and concerned, and the fingers on his forehead cool, a relief.

He was so hot.

Angus thrashed, trying to throw the covers off his sweaty body, but his mother caught his hands.

"Open your eyes. Now."

His lids felt as if they weighed two stone, but he tried to obey. "M-m-other?"

"Aye, 'tis me. I was worried when you didn't come to the hall to break your fast this morning, and now 'tis midday. You're burning up. I must get Lila."

His mother's pretty countenance was blurry when Angus tried to beg his eyes to work, but he managed to grab her wrist. "Nay. No'…Lila. Malcolm, if ye must. No' her."

"Don't be a foolish lad. You're ill, love. Malcolm is away. He went down to the village at dawn after a sick child. He won't likely return until the morrow. Lila stayed for your father."

Angus shook his head, which just made him dizzy. The discomfort in his right side from the past two days was now agony that roared, demanding all his attention.

His eyes still wouldn't work, which only made him feel more disoriented.

Perhaps he was still drunk?

"Nay," he repeated.

Alana snorted, an unladylike sound coming from her. "You're as stubborn as your father."

Then she was gone, her soothing hands making no connection to his face, and the *swish-swish* of her gown's fine fabric fading quickly.

He...hurt.

His heart, his body, his side, and he was so damn hot.

None of it mattered.

Angus didn't give a shite if he was dying, he didn't want to see *her*.

He'd kept to himself over the last two days, only joining his family for one meal.

She'd been there, of course.

Lila hadn't looked at him then, nor any other time in the days that felt like a fortnight. She hadn't tried to come to him, and he'd not had the bollocks to approach her.

Getting drunk in his rooms had helped his heart, and the pain in his side. However, neither condition had given Angus peace since the healer had kicked him from her bed.

His family had left him alone for the most part—and for unknown reasons since they usually loved to smother him, not to mention meddle in his affairs.

Alana had checked on him without ridicule, which had also shocked his senses, and she hadn't brought up the healer.

Angus knew his mother well.

It didn't matter that she'd failed to comment about Lila—she *knew* they'd been intimate and that they'd ended their tryst. The former princess didn't have to read minds, like his Uncle Xander. She was an empath, aye, but she could also read people in a way that had nothing to do with magic.

He was just grateful she hadn't pressed him to discuss it. He wasn't ready to talk, especially to the woman who'd birthed him.

Angus was dying inside.

A little more each day—two or twenty, it didn't matter—that Lila remained at Dunvegan, and he couldn't have her. Or even talk to her. He'd never been more miserable in his life, no matter the short stretch of time that'd passed.

He laughed, but it only made his chest throb and his side sear.

Maybe he really *was* dying.

The pain had been there since he'd stumbled back to his rooms from Lila's guest suite. It'd steadily worsened, and *had* concerned him, but ale and mead had been sufficient distractions. Angus had been hot and cold, but when his limbs had shuddered with chills, ale had helped then, too.

In moments of lucidity, he'd told himself to seek

medical attention, but he would've rather removed his limbs than descend the stairs to Malcolm's surgery — even if he could've been guaranteed *she* wasn't there.

She was everywhere.

When Angus closed his eyes — awake or asleep — all he saw was Lila.

His father was out of bed, and able to walk with the support of crutches — or so he'd heard — but *she* was still in his century.

He wanted her to return to her own time.

Liar.

Angus wanted her to stay in his century.

Forever.

She'd just be required to stay *with* him. For *him.*

As his wife.

Angus snorted out another painful laugh.

His mother had been wrong.

Lila wasn't his fate.

Perhaps that was why he was so broken…heart *and* body. He'd almost been convinced Alana had been correct. He'd started to…hope Lila really was for him. Despite her obvious hesitance in matters of the heart. She'd never wanted to discuss them. Or feelings.

She'd told him many times — before they were lovers — that she intended to go back to the future, but after they'd touched like he'd never touched another lass, held another lass, taken another lass, Lila had been mute on the subject.

He'd been foolish to think there might be a reason for her silence. Foolish to think *he* might be the reason.

Angus had rutted before. He'd never made love until he'd touched…kissed…his little healer. She only wanted his body; the release he gave her.

He'd fallen in love with her anyway.

"Sodding wretch," he gritted out, then groaned. The effort to speak only rolled more agony over his torso. He kicked the thick blankets off, but the movement jerked his enflamed side until he shuddered so hard his teeth rattled as they chattered, which only made his temples throb.

Something was very wrong.

Angus shifted to his side—the one that didn't hurt. He drew his knees up, but that only made his discomfort worse, so he tried to straighten again.

His whole form consisted of agony, and his bladder boomed, too. Of course, he wasn't in enough pain; he needed the result of all the drinking to rear its ugly head as well.

The hangover he could ignore, the urgency of his need to relieve himself, he could not. Not unless he wanted to piss his mattress and lie in it.

When Angus stumbled to his feet, his head screamed, but he made it to the chamber pot and tried to aim so he wouldn't get fussed at for pissing all over the floor.

He kicked empty pitchers, tankards, and trenchers out of the way as he went. He'd taken all his meals, and tons of ale, and some mead, solely in his private domain. He was naked—his normal state of being for the last few days.

His mother was bringing Lila to him, but he had no need to be modest. She'd seen it all, touched it all, tasted every inch of him.

Angus glanced down, studied his manhood. Heated memories didn't even stir it. Damn, he must be sick after all. The little healer usually stimulated his blood instantly.

He gritted his teeth when his right side shot a new arrow of pain, dissolving any memories of Lila's lithe bare form and the magic they'd made together.

Inhaling steadily didn't fix it, and exhaling didn't make it loosen. His head spun and he staggered back to his bed but missed when he reached for the nearest bedpost. He tripped over his feet and went down hard, landing only half on the bed.

The frame hit the edge of his thigh and he scrambled up, trying to avoid landing his bare arse on the stone floor. With a strangled cry, he ended up on the mattress on his right side—crashing his weight on the place that hurt.

White-hot anguish consumed him before blessed darkness swallowed him whole.

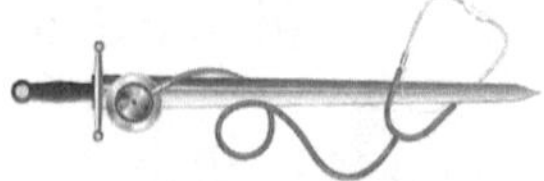

Lila paced her room, biting her bottom lip, but it wasn't doing any good. She'd have to show her face in the hall if she wanted to eat.

Her stomach snarled, roaring that it was done asking politely. She'd skipped dinner last night and breakfast this morning, too embarrassed about what'd happened with Angus to bear dealing with any of his family.

That morning, she'd checked on the laird, and spoken very briefly with Malcolm, but she'd become a sudden room-body since…*the incident.*

She'd helped the clan healer pack his things and seen him off to the nearby village. There was a sick child, and a worried mother had come to Dunvegan for help.

Lila would've liked to see the village, but she'd agreed to stay for Alex. Running away under the guise of work would've been better.

The last two days had been hell.

She'd found a stale bannock in a basket in the surgery and had stuffed it in her mouth when Malcolm had left that morning, but it didn't even *half* cut it. She could feel every missed meal—like enduring the busyness of her residency all over again. She was a fool since the self-famine was voluntary.

As a doctor she reproached herself…Lila knew better than to willingly starve, but she couldn't...deal.

Cobarde. Her belly might as well be yellow.

She'd convinced herself Angus' family knew *everything,* even though no one had been other than their polite-normal-selves when they'd interacted.

Lila didn't care, couldn't look anyone—especially his mother—in the eye.

Paranoid much?

Culpable.

"About so many things…" Her whisper just made her shiver.

She hadn't seen Angus.

Lila wanted to more than…anything.

No matter how many times she denied that it was *true*.

She wanted to rush to him, apologize, declare she'd be honored to be his love…because he was *hers*, too.

Words she didn't have the guts to utter taunted the back of her mind. A three-word phrase, specifically, but it petrified her.

Lila couldn't go home *yet*, but she still *had* to go. Then damn, didn't she want to run to Alana and beg her to send her back to modern-day Scotland *now*?

More than anything.

Because she was a coward who couldn't face her own heart, let alone the man's she'd shattered. She *had* crushed him.

Even if no one had said a word to her, instinct told her they'd been talking *about* her. About *them* and what'd happened.

Guessing all sorts of horrid things, no doubt.

No one might be able to confirm they'd been sleeping together, but like Alana had said that morning days ago on the fighting yard, it was common knowledge how they watched each other. The rest of Angus' family was as annoyingly perceptive as his mother.

Lila crushed her eyes shut and told herself to breathe. She couldn't leave, so she'd *have* to deal with the fallout.

In the back of her mind, it'd always been there. From the start, she'd known no good could come from sex with Angus...other than the intense pleasure while she'd been in his arms.

That was over.

Done.

Suck it up, Lila. Be a hardass surgeon.

Alex could stand with the crutches they'd had made, but she was still training him to walk, so she'd have to '*suck it up*' for a few more weeks.

Claire's sister's husband, Hugh, the laird of the Clan MacDonald, was a woodworker and had made a set of crutches for Lila's patient. She'd met the man and his wife, and their daughter, Brenna, who was almost seventeen when they'd come to Dunvegan.

Juliette, who preferred to be called Jules, was pretty and blonde like her sister, and the dark-haired MacDonald laird tall like the MacLeod males.

Brenna's locks favored her mother, but she had her father's midnight eyes. Her beauty was striking, and her father amusing as he growled away all the curious and appreciative male gazes.

Although, she must've visited often, because she hovered with all Angus' cousins as if unfazed by her father's ire, since only three of them — Claire's boys — were her cousins by blood.

Brenna and Lexi had squealed when they'd seen each other and hugged tightly. It seemed teen girls were the same in the seventeenth century in that way, too. Then they'd gone off together, chattering up a storm that left their mothers smiling in their direction.

Despite the bad clan blood — Claire had explained Clans MacLeod and MacDonald had been mortal enemies for years — the men seemed to be fond of each other, and Hugh had presented Alex with the crutches himself, as if no one else had the right, while Duncan and Xander watched.

They were really too pretty to use, he'd whittled a detailed pattern of swords and thistles, and the craftsmanship was even finer than the little jewelry box Angus had given her.

Her eyes rested on the tiny object still on her bedside table, and her fingers found her Saint Luke medal around her neck of their own accord. Her fingertips brushed her fluttering pulse, and Lila's distress, indecision, only echoed in her temples. Tears pricked her eyes, but she refused to shed them.

She'd hurt Angus, so why was *she* such a mess?

Because she'd hurt herself, too.

Blowing out a breath only made Lila dizzy. Her gut rumbled. Maybe it had started to digest itself.

The knock on her door startled her, and she bit down on a yelp, with only a throbbing lip to show for it.

The thick panel swung open without prompting.

Lila straightened immediately.

Alana's somber—no, downright *worried*—expression could only mean one thing.

"Did Alex fall?" she demanded.

"Nay."

"Then what's wrong?"

"'Tis Angus. My lad fevers. Come, quickly."

Her heart stuttered. "A fever? What...?" Lila swallowed.

Fevers *killed* people in the seventeenth century.

"I do not know. When he did not come down to the hall for yet another meal, I went to his room."

Another meal?

Guilt danced around Lila's chest, tightening things up all over again. Maybe Angus had become as reclusive as her. Like two regular agoraphobics.

She wanted to confess she didn't want to see him, demand that Alana go find Malcolm, but the clan healer was gone, until at least tomorrow.

I'm it.

Besides, she wouldn't lie to the former princess. She wanted to see Angus.

Lila just wished he wasn't ill.

Did I make him sick?

"Lila-lass?"

Alana's concern shook her from her reverie.

"I fear 'tis serious, lass. Come quickly." Angus' mother tugged her arm, and Lila couldn't help but follow.

chapter eighteen

"Angus!"

Alana's shout made fear roll over Lila like a doctor should never feel when assessing a patient. Even if he could never be *just* a patient.

Not after the way they'd touched…what they'd done.

His mother rushed to his bedside, where his large body half-hung off the mattress. He lay on his side, with his right arm at an odd angle as he slumped forward.

Lila tried not to notice Angus was naked and scolded herself for admiring the perfect ass she'd kneaded and caressed so many times.

Very opposite emotions made her flush with heat—embarrassment and confusion among them, and she ordered her feet to carry her to the bed. She scanned the messy room and littered floor as she went.

The stench of stale alcohol hung thick in the air, and pitchers lay on their sides, tankards tipped over.

Two food trays, only one with remnants of a meal, told Lila he'd been drinking a hell of a lot more than eating. The not-eating thing was just like her.

Maybe Angus *had* become like a hermit, too.

Could it be just a hangover?

No way.

Alana had seen many things in her years, and surely wouldn't have panicked over something so trivial.

Something was truly *wrong* with Angus.

Lila's heart stuttered.

"Angus." His mother's voice pleaded now, and she shook her son's shoulder.

"Lila," he moaned.

Lila stilled and had to swallow. Twice.

Alana sought her gaze, and Lila hollered at herself to be a doctor.

Get it together.

Angus was her patient now. Not her...former lover.

"We'll have to move him." She scooted around the oversized frame, and even before her hand hovered over his arm, she could feel the heat from his body.

He always ran warm, but this was unusually so. A fever for sure, a high one.

Lila wished for the modern convenience of a thermometer. Fevers didn't have to be a bad thing, not always. However...he was so hot. Panic inched up from her gut. She had to get it to break and figure out what was wrong.

She couldn't lose Angus.

Not like this. Sure, *she'd* ended things between them, but he'd been down the hall, still real, only separate from her.

Losing him...permanently...wasn't an option.

As a patient, or...as a woman.

"Lila?" Alana's voice jolted her—again.

"Don't worry, I'll figure this out, and he'll be fine."

Angus was a big man, and it took a great deal of strength from both of them to shift him to his back and on the center of the bed. Calling one of his uncles would've only delayed them, so they'd opted to move him themselves.

Alana reached for the blankets to cover him, but Lila didn't comment on the sudden modesty. It wasn't like she was going to confirm she'd seen it all anyway.

Every inch of his skin was on fire when she touched him, but he was also dry—too dry. Not a drop of sweat in sight. That scared her even more. "His fever is high, and he's been drinking too much. He's dehydrated, which complicates things."

His mother shot her a look. "What aren't you sayin'?"

"I need to get his temperature down, but we have to get some fluids in him first. Then I need to figure out what's wrong. I need Malcolm."

Damn, she wished for saline solution and an IV kit.

"I'll send someone for him." Alana hesitated, and

their stares locked. Worry, along with something else, traversed those purple eyes. Obviously, it kept her from dashing downstairs like she should.

Lila wanted to say all sorts of things, but nothing came to mind. Unusual, since she was a gold medalist at professional reassurance. She wanted to break their eye-contact, look at *him*, but as much as she wanted that, she dreaded it. "Go." She cleared her throat when the word came out a croak. "I…care about him, too. He's in good hands."

For some reason she wanted to demand the former princess assure Lila, she trusted her, but the phrase was never born, and Alana disappeared—literally *poofed.*

She'd known Angus' mother could travel telepathically, but seeing her there one moment, and gone the next, was jarring.

Blinking, they'd called it. Angus and Lexi could do it, too.

"Guess it's faster than the stairs."

Lila glanced over Angus, mapping every inch of his powerful form. She sat on the edge of the bed and cupped his cheeks. "Angus. I need you to wake up." She applied pressure on his jaw, but it only elicited a half-groan.

An idea skirted her brain…*kiss him,* it whispered.

"Go to hell," she answered. She wasn't a princess, and her Highlander certainly wasn't a freaking frog. Besides, his lips were cracked, and she didn't want to hurt him.

Lila settled for rubbing knuckles on his sternum.

His brow dipped, and his mouth parted, so she did it again.

"Angus, wake up. Please." For some reason, she wanted to call him, *'my love'* in Gaelic. She sucked in her cheek and bit down. She wasn't doing a great job of holding it together.

Be a frickin' doctor.

If she couldn't manage *'hardass surgeon'* at the moment, she at least needed that.

"Angus." Lila put more power behind his name, and finally those baby blues fluttered.

He blinked a few times, and finally seemed to focus on her. "Lila?" His voice was thick and dry, as if he'd had to perform manual labor to push her name out.

"I'm gonna get you some water, but I need you to tell me what's wrong."

Angus nodded and winced when she stood. The bed moved, and obviously had caused him pain.

"Sorry about that."

Her Highlander didn't answer, but he reached for her wrist when she took a step away.

"Dinnae…dinnae go."

Lila's heart thundered in her ears, and no amount of telling herself to be a hardass surgeon fixed the pain blooming in her chest or the tears that wanted to fill her eyes. "I…You need water." Again, the urge to call him an endearment hovered on the tip of her tongue. She cupped his cheek again because she couldn't help it. Damn her. "I need to get some things from the surgery."

"N-nay. Dinnae…leave me." Angus shook his head, but his expression shouted his discomfort.

He hadn't said *'again'*, but she heard it anyway.

Lila almost lost it.

His needs were foremost, and she told herself not to argue with him. She slid away from the wall and let her gaze skid over the messy room again. On the table remained one upright pitcher. She prayed it wasn't full of ale.

Lila hollered at herself the whole short walk to it, and sniffled.

Don't cry right now.

She had to focus on healing Angus. Hell, figuring out what was wrong, first.

Her hand shook as she poured liquid into a tankard. "Thank God, it's water." She went back to his bed, wincing at his handsome face contorted in pain. "Can you sit up?"

He nodded, and pushed his body up, but it took long excruciating moments, and he didn't get far enough.

"Let me help you." She slid her hands onto his torso, but her former lover hissed when she applied pressure to help him scoot toward the head of the bed. "Where do you hurt?" A scanning gaze revealed no blemishes on his skin, which was even more worrisome.

Angus swallowed and licked his cracked lips, but he didn't answer — as if he couldn't.

She busied her hands by bringing the large cup to his lips. "Slow, okay? Looks like you've had nothing but ale. When you can talk, tell me about your pain."

Lila took a seat on the edge of the bed again but was conscious to do it slowly and not jar him. Being this close made her heart skip, but she had to ignore it.

She was still drawn to him, even when he was unwell. A part of her wanted to throw herself at Angus and demand his forgiveness before she figured out what was making him sick. She wanted to hold him. Wanted him to hold her, no matter inappropriate it was at the moment.

"Here," Angus panted, and his hand tremored as he moved it to his lower right side, beside his belly button.

He lay only inches from her hip, and heat from his fever radiated through her clothing. She needed to get a hold of it immediately.

A dozen things went through her mind, and Lila told herself to focus. She couldn't make a diagnosis without more information. "When did it start? Tell me about the pain. On a scale of one to ten, how bad is it? And don't be a stubborn Highlander. There's only me and you here, so tell me the truth."

He smirked, and she found herself smiling a little.

"I've missed ye," Angus whispered.

Surprise washed through her, and a longing that demanded she be honest with him. "I've missed you, too."

Silence fell, and Angus tipped his head back against the headboard. Closed his eyes.

"Angus." Lila patted his shoulder. "Don't pass out on me, big guy. I need you to drink more water and tell me about this pain."

He coughed a laugh but accepted the tankard of water at his lips again. "Ye've ne'er called me tha'." He only used one hand, so she helped him hold the cup for another drink.

"Well, you *are* a big guy." She smiled.

His lips curved up again, and she fought the urge to kiss him.

Lila cleared her throat. "Tell me about your pain," she repeated and gently moved his hand, starting to palpate the area.

Angus hissed out another breath and cursed in Gaelic.

"Okay, so it hurts there. It also feels swollen. What's your number, please?" She was proud of herself for a steady, doctor-sounding voice.

"Eight...nine."

She met those blue eyes and read the agony there, and in the tremor of his mouth. "When did it start? Do you know how long you've had a fever?"

"'Tis been a bother since…tha' night."

Lila averted her eyes; she couldn't help it. She rechecked his side, coming to a conclusion she hoped was wrong, but as her former lover spoke with labored breaths and drawn-out sentences, her chest filled with dread.

Pain on the right side for days, and it'd started the night she'd kicked him from her bed—of course. He stated that the discomfort had been near his navel at first and slowly worked lower and more intense but had stayed to the right.

Angus had admitted he'd been drunk most of the time, so he wasn't sure when his fever had started, but she would've bet a week's pay it'd been the night before.

He'd said he'd felt hot the whole time as well, and had gone without clothing, but that could be a symptom of the ale and mead, so it didn't help Lila much.

When he'd mentioned the chills, and throwing up, it added up to what she feared, but then again, he'd been drinking a lot, and could've vomited from that, as well.

Even with her guess—appendicitis—not being able to discern when the fever had started for sure was alarming, because if his appendix burst, she could lose him any moment she delayed cutting him open.

Claire scrambled into the room, Alana and Janet on her heels. She had a basket of supplies in her hands, and Lila recognized it as her own. The one Malcolm had given her to use while caring for Alex.

The upside was it was already stocked. The downside, she still needed a few more things from the surgery. Herbs to break a fever, for one. Chamomile should do it, and the healer had it in spades from his fondness for the tea.

"Duncan and Lachlan rode down to the village to get Malcolm. I told them to hurry," Claire said. She shoved flaxen locks from pinkened cheeks and set the basket down next to the bed.

"What can we do to help?" Alana asked. She joined Lila at her son's side and took his hand.

Angus flashed a weak smile for his mother.

"I need some chamomile for the fever from the surgery," Lila said.

"I'll get it," Janet said. She was gone before she could thank her.

Lila took a breath and prayed for strength. To her *lita*, as well as God. Asked both of them to be with her. "I hope Malcolm hurries. I'm gonna need him." She worried her bottom lip, even though she tried to convince herself not to, and that everything was going to be all right.

"What's wrong with my lad?" Alana asked.

"Appendicitis. He needs surgery."

"Oh crap," Claire said.

Lila's eyes found her green ones and she ignored how her heart skipped yet again. Of course, the woman from the future probably knew how serious the condition could be, even if she wasn't a doctor. "It's going to be okay. I promise."

Angus squeezed her wrist and her eyes watered, this time she couldn't suppress the tears.

Why was *he* reassuring *her*?

Wasn't she supposed to be doing so for him?

Lila was the doctor, after all.

Always in control, right?

chapter nineteen

She shouldn't perform this surgery. Lila was emotionally compromised.

Malcolm couldn't do it.

Angus would *die* if she did nothing.

Leaving him was one thing.

Leaving him to die was something she couldn't do, even if she didn't love him.

Lila gasped.

"Lila-lass?" Malcolm's concern was suddenly on her, instead of their patient.

I love him.

Oh. Shite.

The word had, of course, been hovering in her head since she'd kicked him out of her room, but she hadn't had the balls to think it. Not even when she'd been alone with Angus after Alana had come to get her earlier.

Lila had stared at him, talked to him, made him drink water, even cried, but that word hadn't been permitted to make itself known.

Fine time for a revelación.

Maybe if she thought of him as a patient instead of the man, she…loved…she could get through this. However…she *did* love him. Couldn't imagine a world without him.

In the seventeenth century *or* the twenty-first.

If — *when* — she saved his life, could she walk away from Angus?

"I…I'm fine, Mal." Lila flashed a smile for good measure, but it was wobbly, and she had to blink her vision clear. Again.

If she was at the hospital — in Scotland or the US, there was no way in hell her attending would let her perform Angus' surgery.

She was too close to this. To him.

She loved him.

I freaking love Angus MacLeod.

No amount of cursing in English or the new Gaelic words Lila had learned — courtesy of Angus' cousins — would change that.

Her gut tightened, and she had to fight through the constriction in her chest to gulp down air. She put a palm to Angus' forehead.

Still too hot, but his stubbled cheeks were clammy. Proof that at least they'd gotten some water in him before he'd passed out.

Malcolm had made it back with Duncan and Lachlan in less than two hours. She'd briefed the clan healer; they'd compiled all the supplies they'd need and descended upon Angus' room.

While Lila had waited for her colleague, Angus' fever had still raged, but she'd managed to get him to rest. She'd had to promise him to stay by his side before he'd agreed to close his eyes, and when the MacLeod women had given them another moment alone, she'd cried.

She'd not let herself lose it too much, but she'd had to purge a bit. No one had seen her, after all, not even her then-sleeping love.

Alex had come into the room and refused to leave. Even now, he sat in a chair by the fireplace, holding onto his crutches.

The women were there, too, but Janet and Claire were helping, like they had with the laird's surgery all those weeks ago.

Alana hovered between her husband and son, and she'd managed to keep the kids away.

Lexi had come briefly, but her mother had calmed the teary-eyed girl and sent her to stay with the boys.

"I...shouldn't do this surgery." Words fell from Lila's mouth, low and broken.

Malcolm shot her a glance, hazel eyes as wide as his spectacles.

Alana's instant protest was muted by Angus grabbing Lila's wrist.

His blue eyes were full of pain, but his grip was strong for a man with a scary-high fever and in serious physical danger.

Lila needed to get him open so she could see if his appendix was just perforated or if it'd burst. Both bad situations complicated by the 1692 reality.

It didn't matter; the damaged organ still had to

come out.

Her wrist smarted. She'd likely bruise. However, Lila wouldn't have pulled away if she could. She was pinned in place, staring into his handsome face. Even lined with pain, he was gorgeous.

"*Mò gradh,*" Angus breathed.

Her heart tripped into a canter. "Angus." His name was a cracked whisper and she wanted to kiss him again, beg him to forgive her for pushing him away, for ignoring him. Ignoring the heart broken at her hands.

Whose heart was worse off?

The days they'd been apart felt wrong. Days that felt like months, and she hadn't had the guts to come clean about her feelings when she'd had time alone with him while they'd all waited for Malcolm.

Now it was more serious than her earlier cowardice.

Lila was about to cut him open. Not wanting to lose a patient extended to Angus. His father was out of the woods; he was not.

Tell him you love him.

She owed him that, didn't she?

Before she started the surgery.

"Lila, I trust ye. More 'an I've e'er trusted anaone in my life." Each word was pushed out, until Angus' breathing was so labored, she placed two fingers of her free hand at his lips.

He was worse than before. Although he didn't

say so, his pain must be more intense.

"Don't talk, Angus." Her eyes blurred. She couldn't lose her shit before this surgery — the most important one she'd ever performed in her life.

"Lila, I—"

"Angus, please."

The grip on her wrist tightened until her hand turned white, and he tugged until their gazes collided.

"*Tha gaol agam ort*, Lila. *Tha gaol agam ort.*"

Tears already rolled down her cheeks before all the words came out of his mouth, so he hadn't needed to repeat himself.

Lila didn't need a Gaelic translation.

Angus had just told her he loved her.

"Lila?" Alana's voice was soft.

She didn't look away from the man she loved, but he'd passed out. She needed to kick her own ass into gear. Lila leaned over and brushed a kiss onto his mouth.

The room was silent, and all eyes were on her. They'd heard what Angus had just told her, too.

She wasn't embarrassed. She was relieved.

Lila wiped her face and darted to the bucket to wash her hands again. She thanked Claire when the older woman handed her soap and a cloth. Then she grabbed Malcolm's scalpel. "Let's do this."

"Lila?" Alana repeated.

She shot Angus' mother a glance that melted into a locked stare. "I can't tell him I love him until I save his life."

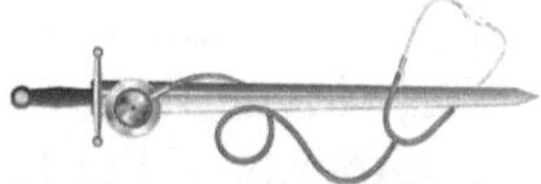

Alana kept him asleep with magic, like she had during her husband's surgery.

Lila had told her to keep an eye on his breathing, but not because she thought Angus would wake. His mother wouldn't have left the room if ordered, so the task would keep her out of the way and allow her to stay with her oldest child.

She was just as determined not to lose him as Lila was.

They both loved him.

Lila suspected the woman had seen right through her plan, but she didn't call her on it.

Alana dragged a chair against the bed and sat next to her son. She stroked his cheek and hair, whispering encouragement and love in Gaelic — or it might've been Fae. The languages were close, and often sounded the same.

Alex watched like a hawk from his chair by the big hearth. The laird was just as invested in her actions as his wife. He looked concerned, but there was no censure in his expression. His brother joined him at one point and rested a hand on his shoulder.

Lila didn't bother trying to fuss anyone out of the room. The MacLeods were too tightknit to listen anyway.

Malcolm followed her every order, and they

worked well together.

She had to compartmentalize to get through this. She couldn't let her love and worry for Angus compromise the movements of her hands.

Dying wasn't an option for this patient.

Angus was the love of her life.

She was an *idiota* for not accepting it.

Lila hadn't decided if she was staying in the seventeenth century, but she couldn't live without him. She added it to the list of things she needed to talk to him about when he woke.

The procedure went quickly and efficiently, better than expected. They'd caught the damaged organ before it'd burst—but the depth of the perforation was evidence she'd opened him up just in time.

She did what she needed to do, and removed Angus' appendix, praying she could control his bleeding. Fears of him needing a transfusion were more serious than when she'd set the bone and sewn up Alex's leg.

Both surgeries could've come with complications. Hopefully, her love would be as lucky as his father. He certainly had youth on his side.

Lila's hand wanted to shake when she started to close his incision, but she steadied herself with a breath and finished the job neatly and quickly. She took a step back, glanced at his face—so peaceful in his repose—and had to suck back tears. Just because she was done didn't mean she could give in to the emotions.

She started to clean up without a word.

Malcolm nodded and followed her lead.

No one spoke right away, then there were soft murmurs from his family. His father was still on the chair, talking to his twin, and Claire and Janet had their heads together whispering.

Alana hadn't left his side, still stroked his face, and suddenly Lila was jealous. She wanted to sit beside him in his mother's stead.

Touch Angus somehow to know he'd be okay.

He'd wake soon, and she could — no, *would* — tell him how she felt about him.

So many things, worries, fears — downright undoctorly freak-outs — swirled in Lila's brain, drowning what little hope was there, despite a successful surgery.

Had the fever come down in time, had the damaged organ been removed in time?

Had he lost too much blood after all?

Was Angus' blood too poisoned with infection?

He could possibly hemorrhage, even though she'd been able to control his bleeding.

Could Lila keep him from sepsis?

Or any other nasty infection. Shock. Staph. Inflammation. Thrombosis. Pulmonary Embolism.

What if he dies?

Lila closed her eyes and banished that last

question. It was too lover—not enough doctor. Her lip wobbled and she bit down on it. She wanted to face the wall because there were too many eyes on her.

People who loved Angus as much as she did and would want answers.

Someone squeezed her hand—and she opened her eyes to violet ones. However, not Alana's.

Xander smiled as he towered over her. His hair was messy, in-need-of-a-trim-long, just like his son's, but Liam had dark locks like his mother. Platinum strands flopped on his forehead, making him look youthful, and contradicting his kind, fatherly gaze. "Worry not, lass. You saved his life. You saved our lad."

Lila blinked tears away. Sucked her cheek in so she wouldn't give into a sob.

Her lover's uncle drew her into his arms. The hug should've been awkward—she didn't know Xander like she knew the women in the family—it was anything but.

Lila took the comfort he offered, hiding her face against his chest to gather her wits. She sure as hell needed to.

Somehow, it wasn't all that odd the tall blond man had read her thoughts. She wasn't irritated, as she usually was. Lila took a big breath and pulled away when she could. She'd tapped back into her strength.

She'd be okay now, as long as Angus pulled

through.

He has to.

Lila exchanged a look with Xander.

He nodded, probably still reading her mind.

"Now what?" Claire broke the silence.

Lila let her gaze slide over the occupants of Angus' suite. His mother was still by his side. His father and Duncan remained like sitting and standing statues, wearing matching expressions—just like they matched. Janet had joined her husband, their hands clasped.

Malcolm, like her, watched all the MacLeods before he looked at Lila, as if he too wanted the answer to Claire's question.

Her eyes drifted to the subject of their collective concern.

Angus had a clean white bandage around his middle—courtesy of the clan healer.

If one didn't know he'd just had surgery, it would appear he was only sleeping, with a peaceful expression. At least he wasn't in pain.

Lila memorized the planes of his gorgeous face. She clung to it, picturing his lopsided grin, and praying she'd see it again. Love and fear warred in her mind—and her heart.

He'll be fine.

Angus would wake up and give her a hard time about staying in bed while he healed, just like his dad.

She wasn't going to lose him.

Lila offered a curt nod to no one in particular and met his aunt's green eyes, since she'd been the one to ask first. "Now, we wait."

chapter twenty

"I love you, Angus."

The warm whisper feathered his face.

He had to be dreaming.

"I love you so damn much, and I was a freakin' fool not to see it. A. Complete. *Idiota. Estupida. Te amo. Mucho.*"

Her repetition shook, suggesting she was crying, and he couldn't have that. Couldn't have his love upset. Why would she be, anyway?

Angus made an effort to open his eyes, but they were so heavy. Slipping back into the veil of sleep was tempting, but he had to *see* Lila.

Look into her eyes when she said she loved him.

Wait…wasn't that the dream?

She *didn't* love him. *Wasn't* his fate.

His mother had been *wrong.*

Right?

"Lila, *mò gradh.*" He forced the words out, but his throat was a desert.

Angus sensed her still.

She must be very close.

His vision continued to be unclear, so he blinked more.

"Angus?" Lila's whisper was now full of

wonder...and worry? "Angus, oh my God! We thought we'd lost you. It's been three days."

"Th...three. Days?"

"Aye, love."

The second voice was his mother. She, too, sounded relieved and concerned, but when his gaze finally focused, all he could see was Lila.

Her face was only a few inches from his. Tears slid down her cheeks.

She leaned forward and settled her mouth over his.

Angus *had* to be dreaming.

The sweet moment was much too chaste and short, then she wiped her tears from his cheeks with gentle brushes of her fingertips.

He didn't mind that she'd gotten moisture on him. He *minded* that she was crying in the first place. He tried to sit up. Agony lanced his right side, but he sucked back a gasp.

"Don't move, love." His mother's voice was low, but clear.

A warm palm settled over Angus' heart on his bare chest. "You had surgery," Lila explained.

Surgery?

He remembered his side hurting.

Other recollections tickled his brain. Being naked and feverish. Lila forcing water down his gullet and interrogating him about his pain.

Malcolm arriving, and his family piling into his

room, but he couldn't be sure about that. It got…fuzzy then.

Although, there was nothing hazy about one memory.

Angus telling Lila he trusted her more than anyone else sounded in his mind, as clearly as if he said it now.

Then…something else.

I told her I love her.

It'd been in Gaelic, not English, but Lila would've figured it out, right?

Had he imagined her saying it back moments before?

Had he still been unconscious?

Aye, 'tis it. Has ta be.

Then again, she'd just kissed him, unless he'd made that up, too. His head and heart reaching for what he wanted most?

Angus swallowed, and the cause wasn't his very dry mouth.

"Here, drink. Slowly." His little healer pressed something cold and metal to his lips.

Chilled water filled his mouth and slid down his throat. It felt so good he closed his eyes and groaned.

"How's your pain?" Lila asked, with an edge of a demand.

Now that his eyes worked, he glanced around the room. Only his mother and Lila were present, but he lay in his bed, in his own quarters. Angus' middle throbbed, especially on his right side, and a wide white bandage circled his waist. "Surgery, ye say?"

Lila nodded. "I had to remove your appendix."

"My what?"

She waved her hand. "Don't worry about that right now, I'll explain it later. Are you hurting?"

Angus sipped more water before she put the tankard on his bedside table. His cheek itched, so he scratched it, and a beard graced his fingers. Three days' worth, as she'd said, because the hair was thick. Asleep for three days?

"Angus?"

"I'm…okay, as ye say."

"You don't hurt?" His mother leaned in, studying him.

He forced a small smile for the woman who bore him. He wanted her to relax. Actually, he wanted her to leave. Angus wanted to be alone with his little healer.

Find out if he'd dreamt her words, and that small kiss.

Alana's gaze was keen and stayed on him too long. Then she looked at Lila, and her shoulders loosened. She gave a half-bow—very beneath her station—and her smile was warm. His mother pressed a kiss to his forehead and looked at his love again. "You two have much to discuss."

Lila gave a laugh that had a nervous edge, and his mother quietly closed the door.

The blue glow fading around the frame told Angus she'd locked it with magic, and probably sound-proofed it, too.

Grab your fate with both hands, my lad. Her voice sounded in his head, and her adjoining mental laughter was smug. She always had to be right, after all.

"She's so…subtle." His little healer averted her gaze and took a big shuddering breath.

Angus chuckled, but agony in his side cut him off.

Lila's dark eyes swung around fast and pinned him where he lay. "Are you all right?"

"I'm braw…" he choked out.

"If you're hurting, I'll give you Malcolm's pain draught." She stood, but he latched onto her slender wrist.

"Wait. I dinnae wanna sleep more." When Angus brought her knuckles to his lips for a kiss, Lila pinkened, and he smiled softly. "She's no'."

"What?"

"My mother…"

"Huh?" She swallowed and he wanted to kiss her throat.

"The woman's many things, but *'subtle'* dinnae be one a' them."

"Oh," Lila squeaked.

He widened his smile. "Lass—"

"Angus—"

They spoke at the same time, and if it was possible, her beautiful olive complexion went even more crimson.

"Ye, first, *mò gradh*." He kept his voice low, but the endearment did as desired, and made her meet his eyes again. Angus wasn't about to forego it. Or back down.

His mother was right; they *did* need to talk. He wanted to explore what his cloudy senses tried to convince him of; he'd heard Lila tell him she loved him. She'd kissed him.

"I…I thought I'd lost you."

"Ye could ne'er lose me." He made sure their gazes remained locked. Angus was making a vow, and he wanted her to know it.

"Before I operated…" Lila was wearing the blue gown he'd seen her in most, and her delectable breasts heaved as she took a breath, making it look like the embroidered flowers danced. "Do you…remember what you said to me?"

Memories of them making love, of her screaming his name teased his mind, but he tried to push them away and focus on their conversation. He could take her later; he needed to talk to her now.

He'd have to recover before he could be inside her again, of course, but he wouldn't contemplate that. Or mourn it. Much.

Those dark eyes stayed locked with his, but Angus' gut told him she wanted to look away and was trying hard not to.

"Aye."

Lila tilted her head to one side. "'*Aye?*' That's it?"

He schooled his expression and nodded, in lieu of speaking.

Her eyebrows drew tight. "Angus—" She looked so troubled, it made his heart skip, but then she opened her mouth, so he let her speak. "You're not going to make this easy for me, are you?"

"Nay." This time Angus gave a little smile; couldn't help it.

She frowned and looked down, as if his comforter was the most interesting thing in the world.

"*Tha gaol agam ort,*" he whispered.

Her eyes shot back to his. Lila swallowed again.

It took everything Angus was made of to resist tugging her down to kiss her throat and take her mouth properly.

Not yet.

He needed her answer.

"Yes, that's what you said." Lila bit her bottom lip, and he wanted to lick the spot.

"Do ye ken what it means?"

She nodded, making her rich dark locks shift over her shoulders.

His heart skipped when she failed to speak, failed to return what he'd said. Had Angus dreamt that she'd said she loved him, after all?

"Me too," she finally said. "*Te amo.*"

"Ye, too?"

Lila glanced away again and took an audible breath. Then she pinned him with those beautiful big brown eyes. "I love you, too. *Te amo.* It's Spanish for the same."

Angus didn't have to pull her to him.

She leaned down, their lips met, parted and their tongues touched in the same perfect moment. She kissed him with the same fervency as always, but this time he *felt* her love.

Whether it was his magic, or instinct telling him so was a mystery, but she wasn't holding back. She was *wholly* with him, heart, body, and soul.

Lila kissed him like he'd always craved.

Although Angus didn't want to, he forced himself to pull away and framed her face, their foreheads touching. He ignored the stitch in his side as he'd moved too quickly. "Ye dinnae walk away from me." He frowned at the desperation of his own statement, but she *couldn't* leave him now.

Not after she'd told him she loved him, too.

Her eyes slipped closed as if she needed a moment, but when they opened, she smiled. It was a small thing, and he would've returned it, had the touch of sadness not been there.

His stomach dipped and he released her so Lila could pull back; sit up.

Was his little healer about to crush him?

"I was a fool to think I could."

Angus swallowed and sucked in a quick breath. Held it, because he was afraid he'd not heard her right. "Meanin'?"

"I love you."

Now his heart was in a full canter, and his head was bound to spin. "I love ye, as well. More than anathin'. My mother said yer my fate. Said so from tha beginnin'. I…I finally believe her."

Lila's eyes misted over, and she dipped down for another light kiss. "I believe her, too."

Angus was still afraid to breathe but let out air slowly. "Will ye stay wit' me? Be my wife?"

Her eyes went wide, and her face was the adorable shade of pink he loved so much. "Did you just ask me to marry you?" Her kiss-swollen lips were a temptation he didn't want to resist.

Angus grinned. "Aye."

She cupped his cheeks. Tugged on his facial hair. "Only if you promise to never let this happen again."

"Tha beard?"

"That, too. But the whole almost-dying thing. Needing emergency surgery and such. Especially the giving me a heart attack afterwards, by not waking up for three freaking days."

He chuckled. "I'll try."

"Then I'll stay and marry you."

Angus tugged Lila back to him and took her mouth.

epilogue

"Just stay off it for a week, and you'll be right as rain." Lila smiled when the little boy's big hazel eyes widened. She made sure the bandage around his ankle was secure and ruffled his sandy hair.

"I dinnae like rain," he whispered.

"Hush, ye wee rascal." His father's deep voice was threaded with amusement, and the oversized Highlander scooped the child into his arms. He inclined his head. "Thank ye, Lady MacLeod."

Heat suffused her cheeks. "Just Lila."

The man nodded again, flashed an auburn-bearded smile, and the boy waved as they went.

Lila leaned back and sighed. She'd already seen a dozen patients that morning and it wasn't quite lunch time. Wasn't tired, exactly. She was invigorated by her new routine.

Malcolm had stepped out, but she had a feeling he'd snuck off with Glynnis, one of the kitchen lasses. A widow about ten years his junior, and they'd been seeing each other for a few weeks.

The man had paced and stumbled over his words when he'd asked if she minded if he took a few hours to himself. Lila had seen right through him.

Time to himself, *my foot.*

However, she was happy for the guy. Glynnis was pretty and sweet. Besides, she was familiar with not being able to wait until nighttime to be with the one she loved.

"Ah, my wife."

Her eyes snapped open and found a grinning Angus, standing in the doorway of her and Malcolm's new clinic. As if he'd read her mind and appeared.

They'd expanded the surgery with Alex's blessing and MacLeod labor. They'd created a separate and private living quarters for the clan healer and built offices for them both.

Of course, they weren't convinced *'clinic'* and *'offices'* were good words, but Claire laughed when Lila had said she'd work on it.

Lila had helped the older man establish actual working hours to see patients, but her colleague also wasn't persuaded to adopt actual individual appointments.

Claire cautioned her not to establish too many modern ways, they needed to remain incognito and not change history.

"Angus!" Lila's heart skipped, from the startle as well as his sexy smile.

Her husband joined her at a jog and swept her off the stool Hugh MacDonald had carved especially for her. Angus' mouth took hers without pause, too fast for her to chide him for moving like that.

Surgery had only been a month ago, and Lila wanted him to take it easy. Winning the battle was a feat she only half-managed, even with Alana threatening to put him to sleep like she had his father.

On a mutual moan, Lila kissed him back, letting him take control and wind his tongue around hers. She got lost in the heat of his chest pressing her breasts flat, the feel of his huge hands on her back and ass. Desire flared, settling low and hot, and she snaked her arms around his neck, pushing closer.

Angus kissed her until her toes curled. She wanted him to put her up on the exam table, take her hard and fast, but anyone could come to the clinic at any moment, including Malcolm.

Lila gently pushed against his pecs until Angus reluctantly broke the seal of their lip-lock. "Take your shirt off."

He flashed a lopsided grin. "Now yer talkin'." He took a step back, obviously eager to obey.

She giggled. "Nay, *mi amor*. I need to check your incision." Like his father, he'd ripped through the first set of sutures, being a foolish stubborn man doing too much.

Lila and Alana alike had chased him off the fighting yard more than once.

Last night the second set had looked good. She wanted to take them out if they were ready.

Angus' expression fell, and she couldn't help but

beam.

"Did you really think I'd let you ravish me here, during clinic hours when I've just finished with a patient? I'm technically between patients, actually."

His sapphire eyes twinkled. "I was hopin' so."

Lila shook her head and bit her lip to fight for a serious expression. "Silly Highlander."

When her husband whipped his saffron leine up and off, her gaze ate up every inch of his defined chest, even if she wasn't supposed to have reprobate ideas in her work area.

"*Mò gradh,* the look yer wearin' dinnae bode well fer me behavin'."

Heat kissed the back of her neck and burned all the way up to her ears, but she couldn't help her smile. "Damn, I love you."

Angus' face lost its amusement and softened. "An' I love ye. Always."

"C'mere. Let me check your side, then maybe we can sneak upstairs."

Desire and intensity reflected in those deep blue eyes. "Aye, my lady."

She snorted. "Now you obey."

He nodded.

Lila arched an eyebrow. "Yeah, when there's somethin' in it for you."

"Ye. I wanna get *in* ye."

Warmth washed over her again, and her lady bits throbbed, heartily agreeing with the man she'd married two weeks ago. "Hmmm, you're making it hard to concentrate."

"Hard." He waggled his eyebrows. "Good." His grin was unrepentant.

She bit back her giggle. "Angus, behave." She slapped his chest, then snaked a hand around his waist to bring Angus in closer for his exam. "Does that hurt?" Lila ran two fingers up and down the tight, dry stitches and admired her neat incision.

"Nay." His headshake made his long sable locks dance.

"It looks great, but let's wait 'til tomorrow to take them out."

"If ye say so."

Lila eyed her husband up and down. "I could get used to this."

"This?"

"The you listening-to-me thing. I think it's a *first*. Perhaps sexual favors were the solution after all? If you disobey, I'll just make you suffer without—"

Angus growled and shot forward, plastering her to his chest and kissed her until she saw stars.

They panted against each other when he broke away.

His stare found hers, eyes burning. Raw with want.

"Okay, you win." Lila fluttered little kisses over his jaw and nipped his chin.

In the end, not only falling in love with the man

she'd married had convinced Lila to stay in 1692. Perhaps his condition had been a part of her decision, though. He would've died had she not been there, and he wasn't the only one.

There were many illnesses and injuries that wouldn't have been diagnosable by seventeenth century standards, even with a skilled healer like Malcolm.

She could help people here, more so than in the future. After all, she wasn't the only gifted surgeon on her end of history.

She was on Angus'.

Lila could save people from dying of curable things.

Angus, and this clinic were her fate.

The seventeenth century was her fate.

Her *lita* would be pleased. She'd drawn on everything the woman had taught her, on everything she'd learned in medical school, and built on them both with Malcolm's knowledge.

She belonged here.

At Dunvegan.

With Angus.

"*Te amo,*" she whispered against his mouth.

"An' I ye, my Lila-lass. *Mò gradh.*"

"Take me to our bed, my stubborn Highlander."

Angus flashed a grin, and planted Lila's mouth with a hard fast kiss. Then he swept her up into his arms, ignored her protest about his side, and did just that.

the end

about the author

   USA Today Bestselling, award winning author of romantic suspense, epic and historical fantasy romance, C.A. loves to dabble in different genres. If it's a good story, she'll write it, no matter where it seems to fit!

   She's a hopeless romantic and always will be. Risking it all for Happily Ever After is what she lives by!

   C.A. is originally from Ohio but got to Texas as

soon as she could. She's happily married and has a bachelor's degree in criminal justice.

She's always writing, and helps small business owners by writing their websites, and she loves it!

WEBSITE: http://www.caszarek.com
EBOOK STORE:
https://www.caszarek.com/ebook-store
PAPERBACK STORE:
https://www.caszarek.com/paperback-store
FACEBOOK:
http://www.facebook.com/caszarek
INSTAGRAM:
https://www.instagram.com/caszarek/
TWITTER: https://twitter.com/caszarek
BOOKBUB:
https://www.bookbub.com/profile/c-a-szarek
GOODREADS:
https://www.goodreads.com/author/show/581508
5.C_A_Szarek
EMAIL: ca@caszarek.com

You can sign up for C.A.'s newsletter on her website, as well as buy all her books!